Christmas In Dixie

By

Beth Albright

Awards & Accolades for author Beth Albright

DOUBLE Finalist for the **RT REVIEWERS Awards**

The Sassy Belles for *BEST CONTEMPORARY ROMANCE*

Wedding Belles for *BEST Contemporary Love and Laughter*

The Sassy Belles WINNER: *Best Debut Novel* from the *Book Junkie Choice Awards*

The Sassy Belles—
Finalist BEST DEBUT NOVEL, RT REVIEWERS AWARDS, 2014
Top Five Summer Pick – Deep South Magazine
Finalist: Best Debut Novel – Book Junkie Choice Awards

Wedding Belles—
Finalist BEST NOVEL, LOVE AND LAUGHTER, RT REVIEWERS AWARDS 2014
RT Magazine Top Pick for August
Nominated for GOLD SEAL OF EXCELLENCE, RT Magazine/August

Sleigh Belles—
Barnes and Noble Bookseller Picks: September Top Pick for Romance

Praise For The Novels of Beth Albright

- Dripping with southern charm and colloquialisms, the novel once again proves Albright's firsthand knowledge of southern culture. *The women in Albright's novels are especially well written*—happy to challenge the status quo when necessary but also aware of that old adage, "You catch more flies with honey." This delightfully campy and romantic read will satisfy fans of Mary Kay Andrews, Alexandra Potter, and Lisa Jewell. **Booklist Review for** *Wedding Belles*

- *By turns tender, witty, steamy, and sharp, Albright's debut novel proves she's a gifted storyteller* with intimate knowledge of southern culture. This charming tale is tailor-made for fans of Mary Kay Andrews and Anne George." –**Booklist Review for** *The Sassy Belles*

- *...with distinct nods to the strength of family, the friendship sisterhood and the indomitable Southern spirit...Albright's first novel is a frothy, frolicking story...*" –**Kirkus Review for** *The Sassy Belles*

- *"Albright good-naturedly displays her inner redneck while steering this giddy Dixie romp with ease-leaving lots of room at the happy ending for another adventure starring these steel magnolias*" –**Publisher's Weekly Review for** *The Sassy Belles*

- **"Readers will find some sexy, Southern fun for Christmas with The Sassy Belles." – Library Journal for Sleigh Belles**

- *"The Sassy Belles are back and sassier than ever! ... With clever dialogue and richly drawn characters, Albright shows once again she's a natural-born storyteller who knows how to pen a charming tale.* Regardless of game-day colors worn, this sexy and fun Southern series will have readers coming back for more!" –**RT Magazine Review for** *Wedding Belles*

- *"The Sassy Belles reminded me that the South is like no other place on earth. Kudos to Beth Albright for capturing its spirit so perfectly in this lighthearted debut novel."* -Celia Rivenbark, New York Times bestselling author of *We're Just Like You, Only Prettier*

Other Novels By Beth Albright

In Dixie Series:

Magic In Dixie

The Sassy Belles Series:

The Sassy Belles

Wedding Belles

Sleigh Belles

Saved By The Belles

Coming in 2015:

Daydreams In Dixie

Stardust In Dixie

Jingle Belles In Dixie

Dedication:

To my hometown of Tuscaloosa, Alabama—You still fascinate and excite me. No matter where I live, I am always so proud to say—My home's in Alabama.

CHAPTER ONE

"Okay y'all—no! No, no! Not there!" Vivi Ann McFadden Heart was standing in the enormous front hall of my freshly renovated southern mansion, soon to be opened as my new bed and breakfast inn, Southern Comforts. She was directing traffic as usual. But this time the "traffic" was the Fru Frus, our decorators, and the frantic shouting of direction was all about the placement of the over-sized Christmas tree.

"Y'all, we need to have that huge tree front and center—I want everybody to see it the minute that front door swings open. It's a statement, you know?" Vivi explained.

"Honey, even a blind man couldn't miss this tree! The damn door nearly knocks it right over the second we *swing* it open. And I for one do not want to hear the descriptive expletives people make when they knock it over comin' and goin'. It's just too damn big, Vivi," Jean-Pierre pushed, his hands placed squarely on his hips. He was one of The Fru Frus—he and Coco owned A Fru Fru Affair, an event planning business.

I could feel the tension rising. And this was only the beginning.

The Christmas season was upon us and I was busier than a rooster in a hen house—yes, I had permanently moved back to Alabama from Hollywood and Vivi's colorful language had begun to rub off on me. The crazy part was that I liked it. I could finally take a long, slow, deep breath now that I was home. L.A never felt like home for me—most of the time it felt like I was just playing the part.

It was tough sometimes too, to pull that off everyday. I never quite understood how a person could feel so lonely in a city of millions of people, but I did. Oh, I had the few people I knew closely through work, but somehow it never felt the same as having family around—and old friends-- friends who have known you nearly your whole life—like Blake, my other close friend, and Vivi. There is a comfort in that. It creates a sense of belonging like nothing else can do. It's a grounding of sorts—to be rooted somewhere. Growing up down south, in Tuscaloosa, Alabama, gave me that grounding and once I came back late last summer to bury Daddy, I felt it lovingly embrace me again. A connected deep root that was still right here—right where I left it.

I never felt planted in L.A. You'll know if you ever leave the place you call home. The whole time I lived in L.A., I always had this feeling under me like my feet were never fully on the ground. I felt unsteady—like I was in a dream. I had a queasiness in my stomach all the time; like I was visiting another planet and soon I'd get someplace where my feet would touch earth again. But the years went by and it never happened. I kept that part of me hidden—especially from myself. But, I've had some time here to feel the difference, to recognize the real me again. To finally touch my feet to earth, the red dirt of the Deep South between my toes--nothing has felt this good in such a long time.

I inherited this monstrosity of a house. It was falling in and had a huge debt attached. But it was my family home, the place where I grew up. The antebellum mansion had deep roots running through the depths of my family, and it held a tapestry of stories and secrets. In the end, I couldn't let it go.

So with the help of my life-long friends, Blake and Vivi, we turned it into a home again. Now it will be a new bed and breakfast inn for Tuscaloosa. The Grand Opening is this coming weekend and we are totally sold out! Vivi and Blake have chipped in along with my two sisters, twins, Abigail and Annabelle. My boyfriend, Jack Bennett chipped in too, and we all own the inn together now. The Southern Comforts Inn, Tuscaloosa's premier B&B. I am so proud I could burst!

"Rhonda! Would you get your ass in here and help us decide," Vivi screeched from the front hall. I was standing right there—right on the other side of the ginormous tree but she couldn't see me. Yes, okay, the tree is a little big.

"It's perfect," I offered. "I like it right where it is."

"In the doorway?" Jean-Pierre asked with his hands on his hips.

"Let's just scoot it back a bit and it'll be right in the curve of the staircase." I bent down to grab the stand and pushed it back with his help. It fit. Well, good enough.

"We're good," I announced. I hugged Vivi, winked at Jean-Pierre and headed back to the kitchen.

"Fine, but now we can't see the front desk. When your guests arrive you'll have to shout from behind the tree…it will be awkward," he sang out but positioned and straightened the enormous fir anyway.

My thoughts were elsewhere and I could tell as I hurriedly left the front hall that Vivi knew I must be up to something in the kitchen. She gave me *the look* as I skipped away.

I went back to the walk-in pantry where I had been when I heard the escalation of the voices yelling over the big tree. I had discovered a treasure. I was counting. Counting the marks indented into the doorframe. The marks had been carved into the wood and next to each mark was a date. The dates were of long ago—another time—when I was a child and Uncle Ron would mark my height along with Abby and Annie's, etching the measurements to be frozen in time just inside the door to the pantry. I stood there, lost in misty memories, counting the marks and comparing myself to my sisters. Abby was always the tallest.

"Honey, just what're you up to—I know that look in your eye and you are up to somethin' for sure." Vivi came sliding into the kitchen without the Fru Frus. "I left those boys to the decorating 'cause I thought maybe you uncovered another secret here in this old house. Did you?"

She moved closer to me and peered inside the pantry door. An instant smile crept across her red lips. She heaved a sigh and rested her head on my shoulder. "This old place is a nest of memories.

That's what was so wonderful about keeping it—every nook and cranny is part of the story."

"The story of what?" I asked her, feeling a salty tear find its way down my cheek.

"The story of you." She smiled warmly at me and squeezed my shoulder before she padded back to the front hall and the Fru Frus. I stood there in the echo of her last words—the story of you—of me. I blinked the salty puddles in my eyes and smiled. In that moment it didn't matter that only two months ago I had found out who my real father was—and the fact that my father wasn't my father at all. It didn't matter that just two months ago I had uncovered my family's dirtiest, darkest secret. My own truth. My mother's sordid affair with her brother-in-law—making me the daughter of the man I called Uncle Ron my entire life. None of the ugly mystery seemed to matter at that moment, as I stood inside the pantry closet, the little girl who only stood so high was staring up at me in my heart and she was so happy that I had kept this old mansion—our family homestead.

Just as I stepped outside the pantry and onto the original wood floors of the kitchen, my cell phone rang, snapping me out of my happy recollections. I raced to my purse that was hanging on the back doorknob. I glanced down at the caller ID and grinned; it was Jack.

"Hello? I don't recognize this number, who is this?" I teased.

"I am looking for the sexiest woman alive, is she available?" He played along.

"Oh I do believe she is, but whom may I say is calling?"

"Tell her it's her lover—and he's ready to love her—now."

"Oooh, baby, well I'll tell her to make sure she's ready and waiting." I giggled. "But I do believe her house is full of –uhm— circus folk right now—let me get them back outside to the tents. Give me—err—her, I mean, ten minutes, kay?"

"I can't wait—the heat is rising if you know what I mean," he oozed.

I felt heat rise up to my chest and cause me to heave a sigh I knew he could hear.

"Better get those crazies outta there—I'm almost there." I heard him laugh to himself as he hung up.

I quickly made my way back to the huge foyer.

"Ok y'all, time to wrap this little party up for the day. The sun's going down and I still have a list as long as my arm. I need to have a little quiet so I can get some things done," I said clapping my hands together as if to scatter flies as I entered the front hall.

"Somebody's on the way and I bet I know whooo-oooo," Vivi sang out grinning at me.

"Oh I see, Miss Rhonda's gotta a booty call," Coco teased. He was Jean-Pierre's design partner at A Fru Fru Affair and his lanky sandy-haired self started twerking right there in front of the tree. "Miss Rhonda, you're all flushed and damp. Must be that gorgeous Jack Bennett. You are one lucky lady," he said, snapping his fingers and moving his neck from side to side.

"Girl, I'll say," Jean-Pierre jumped in. "He is t-totally hot." He smiled as he reached over to the staircase and grabbed his trusty iPad and some notebooks and stuffed them under his arm. "Tootle-loo, sugar." He leaned over for an air kiss and turned to head out the front door, Coco blowing me kisses and prissing out right behind him.

"Call me later, sweetie-pie. I want the naughty details," Vivi winked as she grabbed her purse from the bench near the front door and skipped out right behind them.

The sun painted the evening sky in a low lavender light etched in silvery pink. The early winter dusk gave me a heady romantic flutter as I flew upstairs to my bedroom to freshen up for Jack. He was the real reason I decided not to return to L.A. back in September. I had fallen in love with him the first time I met him, way back over twenty years ago at summer camp. He was a lanky fifteen-year-old that swung across the creek on a vine at Tannehill State Park to splash into me. We lost touch with each other once my parents moved late that same summer to Charleston. Then, when they divorced—life for me became very unpredictable, and after a year at the University of Alabama, I ran off to L.A., married my first husband then divorced him but stayed, trying to make a go of it as a chef in Hollywood.

But, I never forgot about Jack. He was my first kiss. My first love, and somehow he had left an indelible mark on my heart. And honey, nothing in Hollywood could compare to finding Jack again.

After we buried Daddy, and I uncovered Mother's little secret affair with my uncle, then got stuck with my fabulous inheritance—this dilapidated dump—I was furious. Furious with Daddy for leaving this money pit to me, absolutely livid with Mother for keeping my real daddy a secret, and then the dump was dragging me down to an all new low. Then, like a shooting star, Jack arrived and the smoke cleared. My whole world that had seemed so wrong and upside down was at once right and wonderful. I could let out a breath. I was finally home. And the way he found me after twenty years felt like more than just serendipity. It felt like it was always meant to be.

After the insane remodel and restoration was complete, Blake and Vivi and my sisters all jumped on board and we all became co-owners of The Southern Comforts Inn. Our official opening is this weekend with a huge Christmas Gala on Saturday night. I'm so happy. I finally feel at peace with my life. I have my friends, my sisters, and my honey. And I am working on making peace with my mother. Working. Baby steps.

I ran into the bathroom and took off my clothes, spritzed myself with some designer Vera Wang perfume that Vivi had given me as a welcome home present. I leaned over and sprayed my hair upside-down, a trick I remember my sisters used to do in their pageant days. I slid some lipstick across my lips and threw on a loose little silky number in midnight blue lace. My heart was racing. I heard a car pull up near the front porch and I peered out the window down to the front yard and didn't see anything. *Must be the neighbors,* I thought to myself and sat back down at my vanity to brush my hair one last time. Then the doorbell rang. I must have missed Jack's car. I drew in an excited breath and ran toward the stairs. Miss Priss, my big golden Persian leapt in front of me and I tripped, stumbling down the first couple of stairs then catching myself on the bannister. Unfortunately, my grip didn't last in my nervous sweaty palm and I bumped down the last few steps and straight into—Mother. Great.

CHAPTER 2

"Well, I see you certainly weren't expecting *me*," Mother raised her eyebrows as she slid the words out. She was tall, like Abby and overly busty, like Annie. She still had dark hair, though she was in her early sixties. It was teased high and sprayed stiff. She always said, 'The higher the hair, the closer to God.' Her make-up was always right on the border of being too much. But it suited her. It had always been her look, along with a perfectly square purse hanging from the crook of her arm.

"No, how ever could you tell? I dress like this for all my company." I remarked sarcastically. Mother and I were making progress but I knew it would be a long road. Her little secret of the identity of my father, her affair with Uncle Ron with me as the result, well yeah, that kinda has me stuck between wanting to kill her and needing to forgive her. Seeing her standing there in front of that massive oversized tree, her crimson patent Kate Spade dangling from her arm, a silk hounds-tooth black and white scarf tied low, neatly to the strap, she looked as high society as she wanted everyone to believe. Her image was her entire life.

"Let me guess, Sugar. Jack? Is that who you're expecting?"

"No Mother, I'm expecting Santa. He's gonna dig this lacey little number, dontcha think?" She was trying to be the girlfriend so I played along. I had ulterior motives. I wanted her to leave sooner than later.

She stood in the open doorway, the wintry chill of the mid

December air snuck inside, wrapping around my bare arms, reminding me this sure wasn't Southern California. And I loved the wet chill, the frosty breath of Christmastime kissing my cheek.

In Los Angeles, I could never tell what month it was let alone what season. Everyday was sunny and 70 degrees. I know that sounds like a dream but it would get so monotonous. I would find myself longing for a loud thunderstorm, the kind I could remember from my childhood here in Alabama; the kind that shakes your doors when the streaks and flashes of lightening send slivers of magical light illuminating my slumber. The rain beating a rhythmic dance on my windows—it was a slice of heaven in motion. It never rains in Southern California. That's not just a song. It's a fact. And Christmas Day was just like any other—you could spend it in shorts at Disneyland.

The earthy part of me that was so connected to the changing seasons always missed feeling mother Earth move through her elaborate costume changes throughout the year; her colors paraded across my day in the flowers and trees, in the nip of the autumn nights and in the white cloaks of deep winter she spread across her footsteps. It was a feeling I loved and missed—like I was part of the ebb and flow of things. Seasons are the earth's marker of time, and I had missed it deeply into the pits of my soul.

I felt this instantly when I came home in late summer to bury Daddy. Then again when we renovated and saved the old mansion. I felt it even more as Tuscaloosa began to turn the corner into autumn, late September approached and the collective breath of life slowed to an even rhythmical pace. There is something so sweet about the end of summer--a slowing of the frenetic activity, falling into routine, life becomes predictable. Summer barbecues melt into cool evenings by the fire pit, marshmallows dripping into sticky, golden pillows of confection, brilliant leaves tiptoe then scramble across the front yard, into piles lying lazily against pumpkin-littered porches. Glittering sunsets drip into the horizon-- watercolors of lavender and pink yawn and stretch out across an evening sky until the tiny speckles of glitter, the starlight begins to peek from behind the curtains of the early midnight sky. Fall brings a comfort like no other time.

I remember being so utterly happy to be home.

But there was always that little burr under the saddle. Toots Harper Cartwright, my mother, and all her secrets that always floated behind her like a witches cape in the fog of night. And here she was standing in front of the enormous Christmas tree in the front hall, staring at me like we were BFFs. It was awkward. She was trying—so I decided I should too. After all, it was Christmastime.

"Ok, so yes, Mother, Jack should be here any second so you need to run along. I'm sure whatever your little surprise visit is about can wait—nice of you to stop by. Call me next time, m-kay?" I touched her arm and led the way back to the still open door, the chill now causing my skin to prickle.

"No, no baby. I need to tell you something right now."

"Oh, God. What now? I have a hidden brother in the Caribbean?"

"No silly, no more surprises like that! I have a sweet surprise just for you. I wanted to make your up-coming Christmas party and grand opening here extra special."

"So you're fixin' to leave for a three week vacay and can't make it? Aww I'm so sad."

No, Darlin' Mama will be right here front and center. I'm just gonna have some company, that's all."

"Oh lord, who now? I mean, who's left that you haven't already—uhm—had?"

"Well, I just wanted to know if it would be alright if I bring a plus one to the big shin-dig?"

"Sure Mother—but just make sure it's nobody weird, you know, like that idiot you dated from that meditation group after you left Daddy. He, and his dreadlocks, was just nuts."

"Nope I promise I won't.

"Well, who is it?"

"It's a surprise—didn't you hear me the first time?"

I felt a sudden pang of nausea twist in the pit of my stomach. She had a twinkle in her eye that I found unnerving—the creepy kind of unnerving. I had just been sarcastic with her for well over a minute and she never even caught on. She must be deep into love, or lust, with whomever this *plus one* is.

Just then Jack drove up in the driveway just to the left of the wrap around front porch. The evening sky ushered out the last tiny hints of light, the sky now matching my indigo lacey nighty perfectly. I had to get Mother outta here—now!

"Well whoever it is just make sure they're sane and uhm—clean. I really have to go now, Mother," I said gesturing with my head to the left.

"Oh, I see," she grinned. "Alrighty, well, have yourself a marvelous night. Maybe you take after your mother a little more than you know." She grinned a sickening grin and smiled. I cringed at the thought of being anything like her. I knew I could never be.

Smartly, Jack sat in his car pretending to be fiddling with something till Mother's car left the double drive. I saw her wave at him as she backed out. At this point I didn't care if her date was Santa's elf, I just wanted her gone—and Jack in my arms.

CHAPTER 3

By this time I was freezing, standing in the open doorway. But the chill was replaced with a tingle of warmth the moment I saw Jack step outta that vintage crimson Mustang. He looked delicious—and I wanted to eat him up. He was dressed in dark tan soft corduroys, and a navy cotton crewneck sweater. His black wool P-coat swung open down the front. He wore little silver wire-framed glasses, and his dark golden hair was pushed back in a wave over his thick brows. His bright sky-blue eyes glistened when he saw me. He was about six feet three, tall and muscled. A former Alabama football star with his own sports radio show, he looked a little like a young, taller Kurt Russell, dimples and all.

He and I reconnected after more than twenty years. He was my first love—a boy I fell in love with one fateful summer at camp in Tannehill, near Tuscaloosa. He had swung over a creek on a vine to meet me, earning him the nickname of Tarzan.

"There's my sexy girl," he said skipping up the front steps. He pressed his perfect body against mine, his gentle big hands slipping around my waist, the feel of my silky spaghetti-strapped slip sliding across my skin. He shut the door softly with his foot and gripped me tighter kissing me like he hadn't seen me in a month.

"I thought there for a minute, your mother had changed our plans tonight." He kept kissing me as he talked.

"Not a freakin' chance—your hands on me was all I could think about." I opened my mouth and let him in, his hands wandering now.

I felt the light scrape of his five o'clock shadow and his lips brushing against mine as he devoured me right in front of the massive tree. My knees were locked, the heat beginning to travel, down my abdomen with Jack's hands. I wasn't sure we'd ever make it upstairs when all of a sudden Jack lifted me in his arms and carried me up the curved staircase, like he was taking me to his lair. He kept kissing me, his Burberry cologne driving me further over the edge.

It had been a few days since I had even seen him, both of us so busy with the events of the holiday season. Jack had been collaborating with the other sports reporters in town, organizing a shopping trip for local children of poor parents. And I was crazy getting ready for the Grand Opening of the inn and Christmas Gala that was just days away. The Inn was ready and decorations almost finished, except that humungous tree, and the front two rooms. I had run around and turned off most of the lights after Vivi and the Fru Frus left so the mansion was dim. The sconce lighting up the pale yellow creamy walls of the stairs and the tiny white Christmas lights in the garland draped along the bannister led the way to my bedroom. The Fru Frus and Vivi had only just begun to do the bannister.

Jack rounded the top of the staircase and walked softly to my room, laying me on the white plush down comforter, he stepped back from the bed, looking at me intensely. He began to remove his clothes as if in a strip tease for me. This was gonna be fun. I propped up on my elbows to watch the show. He was in a playful mood. He never took himself too seriously, even though he was an award winning former Crimson Tide football star. He paused for a quick second and held his phone—I thought, *you seriously can't be texting right now*—but within a second some sexy Barry White was humming from his device. He grinned as he pulled his sweater over his head, removing his glasses first, setting them down on my bedside table. Next he dropped his hands down to the first button on his white oxford, moving his hips slowly to the next and then the next, each button had me inching closer to the edge of the bed—it was impossible to keep my hands off of him but I let him continue the smoldering show. Soon his rippled gorgeous chest was fully exposed. He removed the shirt completely his hands falling to the button of his pants, the bulge already visible. He opened the top of his pants, sliding down the zipper in one quick move. He pushed his pants past his hips revealing black Calvin Klein boxer briefs over taut muscular defined thighs. I was salivating.

Jack stepped out of his pants and moved closer to me. I was never good at that *look but don't touch* rule, I cupped my hand around his hard package—just as he tripped over his pants, falling over on me.

"Oh my God, sorry, baby."

Barry White kept singing from the phone speakers.

I could barely breathe. Jack had me so hot. And he was on top of me, exactly where I wanted him. I slid my foot between his legs and helped his pants fall to the wood floor. His lips tasted my shoulder, kissing me lightly then with more determination. He slid his naked body into a better position on top of me, bit my spaghetti strap and moved it with his mouth off my shoulder. I slid my arm up and out of it as he moved across my breasts, kissing my flesh as he traveled. He did the same to the other side. He bit the other strap and just as he tried to move it off my shoulder he stopped abruptly.

"Oh God, it's stuck," he mumbled.

"Not yet, but I have high hopes," I teased.

"No. I mean it really is, the strap is thuck in my teef."

"Oh no! Can you get it out?" I totally *never* thought I would be saying *that* to Jack.

"No. It's thuck under my temporary cap. I just got it yeferday and it must have a gap."

Poor Jack sounded so awful as he tried to speak with my nighty strap trapped in his mouth.

"I'm not gonna be able to get up unless I take vis fing off of you."

"Now that's a ploy, to get me naked, I've never heard." I was trying so hard not to laugh, but I was about to burst. Here was sexy Jack, his undies half off, ass exposed, lying on top of me with my spaghetti strap caught between his teeth; me underneath him, one arm out of my left strap, my left breast exposed, and Jack talking like his mouth was full of mush.

"What can I do? Tell me what you need me to do," I pleaded.

"Oh what a great fwuestion vat would've been," Jack said playfully, even though he had my nighty trapped in his upper jaw. "But for now," he continued, "so I von't voose the crown, fry to wriggle out of the frap so ve can stand up." Jack was mumbling so much now as the strap had become deeply wedged under the edge of his tooth.

Ok let me try to pull my arm under you and then slip it out." I gave it a pull but I felt like I was fixin' to break my arm.

"Thweetheart, we gotta vet you outta your gown—Jack was mumbling so badly now with the mush mouth I could barely understand him.

"Jack, I can't get it out. It's stuck."

"I know, the gown is thuck too, so we gotta vet you arm out or neever of us can vet up. I don't wanna yank my damn thoof out, baby."

"Alright, alright, lemme turn the other way and see if I can get my arm out that way." I gave it a heave and I heard a little rip. "Oh no, my favorite nighty...I think I tore it."

"Honey if ve hath to tear it oth you I gotta be able to vet up so what-ether it thakes. The two of us can't valk around togever like vis. It's alreavy gonna be real vad when I arrive at the ventist with this little numver hanging from my mouf."

I couldn't help it any longer. I burst out laughing as I finally slipped my other arm out and he lifted up just enough for me to roll out from under him.

"Oh fank God, lemme vet da fissors."

"No! You can't cut my pretty nighty! Just, like, lemme think--stuff it under a hat!"

"Seriously? I can't walk around with vis fing voing vup my face under a vat. We gotta cut it out. I vromise I'll vet you a vew gown. Please, baby."

I looked at Jack, standing there, nearly naked, the ripples of his thighs visible in the moon-shadows cast through the window at the side of the bed. I heaved out a sigh. I got up from the bed, totally naked myself now, and walked over to my dresser and retrieved a pair of scissors. I sauntered back to him smiling. I had to admit, it was funny.

"Ok, Sugar, stand still," I said. I felt a pang of sickness churn as I snipped the lacy sheath from Jacks mouth, it dropping to the floor. He placed his hand on my bare smooth hip and let it travel up to my breast.

"I can't stand you being vis close to me wivout clothes, I can barely take it—if this damn thing wasn't trapped in my mouth, I'd make love to you all night." He sounded better since the heaviness of the silk wasn't pulling his lip down to his waist. I reached for the sheet and pulled it to me, wrapping myself in the cool cotton.

"Go. You have to call the after hours number and get to your dentist. That dark blue strap is nearly invisible in the moonlight here, but it's gonna look like a helluva piece of spinach come tomorrow morning. And I know you've got that charity shopping trip after the kids get out of school." I pulled the sheet tighter around my body as we headed back down the stairs.

"So baby, I owe you," Jack said looking like he had a tuft of cotton stuck in his upper cheek. He was like a wounded child; his wagon just fell apart—in my bed. We made our way downstairs.

"It's ok sweetie, I know you'll make it up to me—I'm actually really looking forward to it. Get going before it gets too late. Call me when it's all fixed." I leaned over and kissed his rough cheek, his late day beard sexy and masculine. He reached around my back and squeezed my rear, kissing my neck as he turned to leave. I shut the door and moved into the dining room to watch him leave through the window. I was in deep. I loved Jack, pure and simple. I watched through the foggy cold glass until his car was out of sight, then, made my way to the kitchen, still wrapped in my sheet, to get some iced tea. We drink iced tea year 'round down here. Even in the dead of winter, it's the year-round house wine of the Deep South.

I closed the refrigerator door and stood there lost in thought. Just then—KNOCK! *KNOCK, KNOCK!* Someone was banging on my back door to beat the band. And I was standing in nothing but that sheet. I peeked out the window. It was the older lady from next door, Gladys Haygood. Relieved, I opened the back door.

"Good Lord, honey! Next time y'all need to make sure those windows are closed a little tighter, with all that, '*It's stuck, I can't get it out*' shit. I thought I'd have to get Harold out for a while, if ya know whatta mean." She was about seventy-five, chubby and gray with a wide warm smile and a twinkle in her gray-blue eyes like she was up to something—and she usually was.

"Oh, Mrs. Haygood, I am so sorry it—it, uh wasn't what you think. I, well, he…"

She cut me off. "Oh dear, you don't need to explain to me—I was adventurous in my younger years too. Still am. Wanna meet my Harold?"

"Oh no—I'm not, uh, dressed," I said gesturing down to my sheet.

"Oh honey, Harold's not my husband. Benny been gone for years. No, Harold is my little friend. Some nights he sees a lotta action, like tonight. Whew! You two were sure puttin' on quite a show."

"What kind of little friend?" I cringed when I asked. I then suddenly wished I hadn't. But, it was too late.

Mrs. Haygood leaned over to me and whispered, "You know, the kind that comes with batteries and shakes," she laughed. "I just wanted to let you know, close yer windows, child--you gonna have the whole entire neighborhood hot and bothered. Merry Christmas." She waved over the back of her head as she sauntered home, through a grove of century old magnolias. I watched her to make sure she arrived safely to her back porch.

What a woman. I hoped I'd still be that active when I was in my seventies. She was a sight. I knew I *had* to invite her to the Christmas Gala. She would be a fun addition to the guest list. Oh! The guest list. I had planned to check it earlier, but then Jack called. I padded to the front nook behind the staircase and sat down at my desk tucking in the sheet under my arm. I opened the drawer and pulled out my register and scanned the lists. We had a guest list going for the Gala and a hotel register for the inn. Booked solid. I loved seeing that. Until one name caught my eye. Marci Miller. My eyes froze on her name.

A lump formed in my throat and my gut. I knew that name. Marci was Tuscaloosa's Miss everything once upon a time. Back when I was at the University of Alabama before I ran off to L.A. with Jason, my first husband, Marci was head cheerleader for the University of Alabama, and Miss Tuscaloosa—our representative to the Miss Alabama pageant that feeds into Miss America. She was the most gorgeous girl I ever saw, long very dark bouncy hair, perfect alabaster skin, ocean blue eyes with eyelashes so long they looked false but weren't. She had a big bust and long legs and I wanted to be her. She was registered with her maiden name. Not married. What in the world was she doing staying here? She had family in town so maybe she was just excited to see the old mansion restored. It had once been such a mainstay in Tuscaloosa.

But that wasn't the real reason my eyes had frozen on her name.

Marci wasn't just Jack's college sweetheart—she was Jack's ex-wife, the one he caught in bed with two other men. And she was booked in my inn—for opening weekend, which meant only one thing. Marci would be at my big Christmas Gala. With me. And Jack.

CHAPTER 4

The early morning light of mid December splashed across my white comforter. The skies were a crystal blue, the stick trees of winter etching shapes into the puffy white clouds. I stretched and yawned and tried to coax myself out of bed. Even with the gorgeous outdoors and perfect crisp temperatures beckoning me, I didn't sleep well and the exhaustion was clinging to me in all the wrong places. All I could think about as the night wore on was Marci Miller. I wondered why she was booked opening weekend. What did she want?

Something inside me gripped at my chest and my heart raced every time I felt like I might doze off. Images of Marci flirting with Jack would float in and jar me awake. Suddenly I heard a rapid knocking at the front door. Ok, up and at 'em. I *had* to get up now. And maybe for a second, I would stop thinking about Marci Miller.

"I'm comin'! I'm comin!" I pulled on my robe and tied the sash as I bounded down the stairs and flung open the door.

"Well, Miss Rhonda, it looks like I have disturbed you this mornin'—I'll jes come back later." Drew Dawson, of Dawson Diggs was standing right in front of me looking like he was ready to get to work. The thing was he had finished all the work way back in September. Drew was my contractor, and I totally considered him family.

"Hey Drew! What in the world are you doing here? What a nice surprise!" I was genuinely happy to see him—an old familiar face—standing on my front porch. He was in his mid-forties and graying sparkles glistened in his otherwise light brown hair. He was not too tall but very sturdy, dressed in blue jeans and thick plaid flannel shirt. There was the ever-present twinkle in his soft brown eyes. His hands were on his hips, his weight on his left hip. He was just a sight for sore eyes. His help and friendship really saw me through a super difficult and highly emotional renovation on this place, and he worked double-time finishing under the wire. Drew was my ally. He always would be.

"Get in here," I invited, "it's nippy out there this morning." I backed up to let him step inside.

"Oh, I love these Christmassy temps outside, keeps the old blood pumpin'," he laughed as he stepped inside the front hall.

"Man, that is a helluva tree, Miss Rhonda. You better hope none of your comp'ny is a fatty, they'll knock this here tree right over," he snickered to himself looking up to the top of the tree.

"I know it, but I love it so I'm gonna keep it there and cross my fingers. It makes a statement," I offered smiling as I closed the door behind him. "So just what do I owe this spectacular surprise visit?"

"Well, I was a thinkin'—how 'bout we get this yard real decorated and landscaped for the big grand opening? I got yer invite over the weekend and thought you might need it. I know them media folks are gonna cover this and that will be some good publicity for the new inn. Since it's an historic home it's gonna get lots of attention, ya know?"

I had to admit, I hadn't even thought about the yard. We had been so consumed with the Gala; the outdoor decorations never even came to mind. With the big event just days away, Drew was right. I needed help.

"You're right, Drew. The outside is where we need the most help right now. Vivi and the Fru Frus are working their magic inside, I got the menu covered and Blake has been handling the minor details, like all the invitations to the media. So Drew, as usual you are my lifesaver. What do you have in mind?"

"Remember that dude that did all the original landscaping—my gardener? I can get him real cheap this time a year and he'd love the work. You know he's kinda down and out and the work always perks him up. He can do whatever you want: lights, extra trees, a Christmas scene of some sort--whatever you like."

I recalled the scruffy man that did the original work when we renovated. He worked hard but I never even spoke to him. He had a long dark copper beard and wore a huge floppy hat. But I already knew I liked him—he created my dandelion garden in memory of Granny Cartwright right up near the back kitchen door on the side of the wrap-around porch. He had amazing attention to detail. And he seemed to just know what I liked. I'm sure Drew helped him a tad in that area. All that pink and white striping he used and that silly dandelion garden—it was all so special and so personal. Granny Cartwright always told me dandelions were not weeds, they were wishes—just close your eyes, wish and blow. That old gardener seemed to be able to hear my heart when he made me that garden.

"Yes, I do remember him," I said all excited. "Let's get with Blake and Vivi and get us a plan going then you can let him know, okay?"

"Sure will. Lemme know when y'all can meet and I'll drop back by. Sorry for the early morning surprise visit. I just wanted to see if I could get this poor guy some work. He's a good guy and I sure think we could use him."

I loved how he said, 'we'. We were all in this together.

"What's his name? I never even knew his name."

"I call him Gus. He never told me anything but Gus. But I have a feeling there's maybe more to that name than he wants to say. He came by last summer looking for work. He's a little eccentric, a loner I think, but he's really fantastic at what he does and he's pretty cheap too. I'll tell him the good news. Call me when y'all are ready to plan. We need to get moving on it by tomorrow. The Gala is Saturday so we only have a few days."

Drew was right. It was Monday and my calendar this week was beyond full. Check-in for the inn was to be begin on Friday night. Jean-Pierre and I had already begun to fill the freezers.

"Alrighty, I'll gather the girls and call you ASAP." I hugged his neck as he turned to leave. "I'm so glad you were thinking for me—I guess some things never change." I smiled and shut the door behind him. I realized right then that this was it in a nutshell. My friends would always be thinking about me. It was one of the things I missed most when I was in L.A. I love this small tight community I was in now, here at home in Tuscaloosa—and Drew Dawson was most definitely in that circle. Maybe I needed Gus too. That yard was nearly an acre and come spring I'd sure need the help. And I was pretty sure Gus just might need all of us too. Drew sure seemed to want to help him out. And 'tis the season to be inclusive.

Taking in strays—Granny Cartwright was the ringleader in that area. Her door was always open. They always did make the best family—ones I created on my own.

Yep, I think maybe Gus could use some family too.

CHAPTER 5

I ran upstairs and showered and dressed, calling Blake and Vivi for a quick conflab. A conflab in the Deep South is when you gather to discuss. And we most definitely needed a conflab. I told Vivi to grab the Fru Frus and meet me here at the house. They were all here before I knew it. We gathered around the large banquette in the huge kitchen. Hot chocolate and coffee along with fresh orange cranberry muffins I had made the day before were all placed in the center of the table and I had a fire going in the fireplace.

Every room in this historic house had a fireplace—it was one of my favorite features of the house.

It was already looking cozy for the season but we still had so much to do. They all arrived about the same time.

"Hey girl, y'all come on in. I got food and drink ready to go and ideas are flying around my head already," I said leading the way into the bright kitchen and we all scooched in around the table. I filled them in on what Drew suggested.

"Well, I for one, think we most certainly need to add more trees," Coco offered. "Maybe even a wintry Victorian scene, y'all know, with carolers in costume."

"Ooh, yes, I just love that idea! How 'bout it Blake?" Vivi shot.

Blake was the smartest one of the bunch so I valued her opinion even more than she knew. She had been my best friend along with Vivi when we were all in junior high, long before my life fell apart, mother and daddy moved us to Charleston, then divorced and life as I knew it disintegrated. She was an attorney and very logical. Most of the time.

"I think it's a fabulous idea! I just wanna make sure we keep it classy and don't overdo it."

"You mean like if we decided to put us a real life manger scene complete with live animals?" Vivi blurted, only semi-sarcastically.

"Exactly. That would be defined as over the top." Blake threw it back as if in rhythm with her. And they were in their own rhythm—a cadence developed over twenty something years as best friends. I was sad I had left sometimes. My experience in L.A. was good—and different, but a life-long friend is so priceless. A life built around the people who are important to you is priceless. They both treated me like I had never left, but they shared experiences I will never know. Memories I never made. It always had me thinking.

"I think the carolers will work, but the rest needs to be completely classic, lighted trees with white lights only, lots and lots of crimson, you know, kinda like Dickens Downtown, only we'll have it here in the front yard." She smiled and took a bite of her cranberry orange muffin.

"Well, I think that idea is fabulous, myself, but honey, did you even consider that we're gonna need us some actors—actors who can sing?" Jeanne Pierre shook his head at Coco. He was the more realistic of the two business partners. They were hilarious, prissy decorators and caterers. They were a huge help during the renovation and then they drove out to L.A. to finish up my commitments there. They even drove a truckload of green tomatoes to fry so my catering business would have the promised items. They are most assuredly in my little circle here. I loved them both to pieces and I had to admit, Jean Pierre did have a point—live people—performing in the yard. It might cause quite a challenge.

"I have a great idea!" Coco interrupted enthusiastically. "Why don't we get some elves to be the servers, or they could even park cars! I love my own idea!" He laughed out loud.

"Great! Jeanne Pierre dripped with sarcasm. "Now we're gonna need a sleigh full of little people. I don't even know any little people personally, do y'all?"

"No, not personally. But there has to be like a place to get some. Right, y'all?"

"Honey, there are no stores where they have little people for sale—it's not like we can go shopping for some elves."

"No, silly, you know--like an agency—like an acting agency that specializes in them."

"In case you have forgotten, we are not in Los Angeles anymore. We are back in Tuscaloosa, Alabama and I cannot recall *evah* seeing little people *agencies*." Jean Pierre rolled his eyes and shoved a muffin in his mouth.

"Let me see, what would it be called—'*Oompa Loompas Are Us'?*" Vivi had to join in.

Everyone laughed.

"My Gosh, y'all—it was just an idea. Jeanne Pierre you are such a Debbie Downer." Coco huffed and sipped his hot chocolate, a mini marshmallow clinging to his upper lip. I liked the idea of having people parking cars and serving drinks and hors d'oeuvres. This sent my wheels churning.

"Maybe we could hire some gorgeous Alabama football players to come by and dress up in Tux and tails to park cars and serve. Even some hunky Bama frat boys," I offered.

"Oh, honey! I love that idea! Yes, I'll personally assign myself to this one." Blake wrote in her leather journal then tapped her pen on the page. "Brilliant idea!"

"Jeanne Pierre," Coco commanded. "Com'on, honey, walk outside with me a minute and let's get the layout of just what we want, strolling Victorian carolers and all. We need to plan just where it's all gonna go." Coco smiled and scooched out of the banquette, followed closely by Jean Pierre, his trusty iPad in hand. They headed into the front hall through the dining room.

"Good God, y'all! That tree is co-razy big! Whew! I guess it sure shouts Merry Christmas!" He giggled as he squeezed past the enormous Noble Fur. As soon as the boys were out of earshot, Blake and Vivi eyed me.

"Okay, girlie, do tell. I know Mr. Bennett was due here last night and somebody had herself a private little party, I'm sure. Time to spill, Sugar." Vivi patted the now vacant seat where Coco had been sitting and raised her copper eyebrow at me.

"Yes, honey. We need to know all the dirty details." Blake grinned and took a sip of her now cooled coffee.

I reached over to the coffee maker and grabbed the little pot, an antique like most things in the house, and poured myself a cup, refilling Blake's pink cup while I told the story of my surprise stripper—who then needed an emergency dentist.

"Oh, my word, he certainly knows his way around a bedroom," Vivi bit into her muffin and chewed slowly--lost in an image I was sure.

"And around a woman's bare body. But then he got stuck," I snickered to myself.

"Stuck?" Blake popped, now both of her brunette eyebrows raised.

"Are you kiddin' me? Stuck—like *stuck*?" Vivi raised both eyebrows this time too.

I laughed at the memory of Jack with my silk nighty stuck in his tooth. I explained it to the girls.

"He what? He was undressin' you with his mouth? Oh Rhonda, I would have never guessed that. Jack seems so straight-laced. But honey, sounds a little kinky. He is suddenly *much* more interesting." Vivi leaned in and purred.

"But yes, in such a good way," Blake added. I was pretty sure she and Sonny had some pretty, uhm, *fun* romps themselves. Blake winked at me assuring me I was right. She knew what fun could be had under the covers—and out.

"Well, then, we had to cut the nighty out of his mouth so he wouldn't be prancing around town with midnight blue silk hanging from his lips."

They both burst out laughing.

"He sent me a text this morning. I wish I could have been a fly on the wall as he explained to his dentist just how lingerie found it's way into his mouth."

"Knowing Jack, he flashed his sexy little grin and the dentist just knew."

"And then slapped him a high five."

I stopped in the middle of all the laughing as thoughts of seeing Marti's name in the hotel reservation list crept back into my head.

"What is it, Rhonda? Everything's ok with you and Jack, right?"

"Oh yeah, we're perfect," I said. My tone had obviously dropped, putting a damper on the upbeat conversation.

"Then, what? What's that look?" Vivi asked concerned.

"Y'all remember a Bama cheerleader named Marci Miller?"

"Oh honey, who could forget her? She was head cheerleader our senior year, then Miss Tuscaloosa. She was the big star. Rhonda, you had already left, I think. Blake and I had just heard you were at Alabama but we never found you since y'all had moved back from Charleston. I mean it's really not our place to say but you probably already know it."

"What?" I pushed.

"Well, she and Jack were quite a thing. For quite a long time." Blake looked suddenly serious.

"I know that. Jack told me after I decided to keep this house and stay in Tuscaloosa. That was his longest serious relationship."

"Why are you thinking about her? He didn't bring her up in the middle of his midnight snack with your nighty did he?"

"Of course not but lemme show y'all something."

I got up and walked over to the guestbook that was still lying on the kitchen counter from last night. I turned the crisp pages until Marci's name appeared. "Look," I said. "Read this."

Blake grabbed the book and pointed to Marci's name. "What in the world is she doing coming here for the grand opening?" Blake questioned.

"Last I heard she was married to a millionaire real estate developer and living in New York," Vivi elaborated.

"Yeah and her new last name was Bramhall. She's registered here with her maiden name," Blake noticed. "I wonder if Jack knows she's coming to the big grand opening? Has he mentioned it to you?"

I felt my stomach twist and my breath freeze. "No, he hasn't," I managed, finally getting my words to squeeze past the lump forming in my throat. The thing is they didn't know what I knew about Jack's past. The first night we were together at the radio station party at my sister's—when I answered the door with mashed potatoes dripping from my hair—late that night Jack and I had sat on my sister's front porch and talked for hours, getting caught up. He had told me he had been married, to a girl he knew from school. They had broken up but after he went to play pro football for New England, he ran into her. They had what he described as a quickie marriage. The reason for the break-up? One day he came home to find her in a threesome.

After the divorce she married a former football player who went into real estate development. It wasn't until after I decided to stay in Tuscaloosa he told me it was Marci. I guess he thought I should know since her parents still live here. He knew she'd surface eventually. It's just that she's coming up for air right here, right under my nose, as a guest in my inn. The knot in my gut was growing. I knew Manri wasn't just a college girlfriend; she was Jack's ex. I decided to wait to tell the girls. I knew I had to talk to Jack first.

Blake and Vivi took a last sip of their coffee and hugged me, one after the other.

"Look, honey. We got'cher back. Marci was always a little uppity for my taste. And no one could ever believe how she could cheer while her ginourmous boobs stayed perfectly still. It was a t-total miracle she didn't keep two black eyes. We all thought she had been to Birmingham to see *Dr. Lord, have mercy, are those things for real?*" Vivi laughed out loud and touched Blake's arm as Blake broke out in laughter.

"Oh I totally remember that," Blake added. Phi Mu, mine and Vivi's sorority voted her Barbie of the year, since she looked so plastic. Vivi's right. She's probably just here to see her parents and heard all about the new inn. She always did have to be at the top of any social list. We'll help you watch her. Relax. You have a lot on your plate, missy. The next few days are gonna be a blur. With the Gala on Saturday night, we only have four full days to pull it all together."

I knew they were right. I drew in a deep breath and closed the hotel guest book, clutching it to my chest as I headed over to the large kitchen drawer to put it away. "Y'all go on. I'll meet you at the front door. We can go check on the guys and get this show rolling." I turned and made my way over to the back door near the oversized sideboard as Blake and Vivi left the room. I knew I had to get a grip, as Granny Cartwright used to say. This Christmas season was gonna be one of a kind and deep down I was just giddy. I had to let this Marci thing go.

Finally, I was fixin' to have my first real Christmas—in—I couldn't even remember when. The grand opening of the Southern Comforts Inn was coming right along with Santa Claus and with the Fru Frus and Vivi in charge of all the decorating for the big Christmas party, and of course, me fixing all the food, honey this was gonna be a Christmas shin-dig the south would never forget! I had to believe it. But just as I shut the kitchen drawer, Vivi hollered from the other room.

"Rhonda! Get in here quick! You ain't gonna believe who's standin' on your porch."

I ran in and peered out the floor to ceiling window next to Vivi. Our breath fogged up on the frigid glass. Standing on my front porch, four days before my grand opening was Marci Miller. And her enormous breasts!

CHAPTER 6

I stood next to Vivi, motionless. My eyes burned, and my stomach churned. What was Marci doing here now? Four days early? And I barely had my make-up on. You just don't answer the door down south with no make-up on. Never. Especially when Marci Miller is at the door. She stood in crimson suede pumps, winter white wool pants and a matching tight knit V-neck sweater, her cavernous cleavage spilling out of it. Her shiny hair fell in long dark bouncy waves over her shoulders, cascading down her small shapely arms. A perfectly square crimson Coach bag hung from her forearm, several gold charm bracelets flickered in the morning light from her wrist. She was perfect. And it made me nauseous.

"Well, aren't you gonna open the door?" Vivi pushed.

"You can't just act like you don't hear her. She must've seen you two idiots peeking out the window by now," Blake smirked.

I looked at both of them. Knowing they had no idea the depths of the relationship Marci and Jack had years ago. Knowing they had not even an inkling that Marci and Jack were married at one time—they could have no empathy for my sudden need to puke. They couldn't begin to understand. They sure didn't know she had been found by poor, sweet, Jack—in his bed with two other men, at the same time! If they knew, they'd wanna kill her too.

"Sweetie, you're as white as a ghost. You look like Vivi always looks!" Blake snickered to herself. Vivi was so white she was almost blue, covered in freckles with a crown of dark copper frizz, her ruby red lips and bright green eyes adding that touch of perfection. Blake was tall with lovely light brunette waves and blue green eyes and perfectly tanned milky skin year-round. But none of us, in all our glory looked like the overdone movie star that Marci resembled.

The doorbell chimed again, followed by a knock.

I swallowed hard and moved over to the door from my vantage point where I had been in a stupor at the window, looking at her. In a split second I wondered if she had heard about Jack and me and that was why she was here. She wanted to check me out. And then all I could think of was that I looked pretty plain Jane compared to her. I hesitated a second too long.

"Oh, I'll get it myself," Vivi huffed.

"Good idea. Get rid of her," I begged. "I'm not prepared to meet her right now."

"No problem, girlie—I got this." And with that, Vivi moved in front of me and I slid behind the large front door like a little child.

"Hi may I help you?" Vivi asked, acting like she had never seen her picture and had no idea who she was.

"Yes, I'm here a few days early. But I was wondering if I could check the accommodations. I have a reservation for the Grand Opening this weekend," Marci said, her velvety voice like Lauren Bacall.

"Oh, well, we're not officially open yet as a hotel. Check-in actually begins on Friday at noon for the Grand Opening and Christmas Gala on Saturday. Right now this is still a private residence so today it won't be possible. I'm so sorry." Vivi asserted.

"Are you the owner?" Marci pushed.

"Actually, yes, I *am* one of the owners. Did you need anything else?" Vivi was pushing her to go.

"Uhm, well, I was hoping to meet a Rhonda Cartwright. Is she here at the moment?"

"No, she stepped out for a meeting. We certainly look forward to seeing you on Friday. Thanks so much for stopping by. You have a good day now." Vivi smiled and shut the door. I loved how Vivi operated. I was still standing behind the door and grinned as Vivi confidently placed her hands on her hips.

"Well-played, mama! You are good!" Blake high fived her as we all giggled. I peeked out the window and watched Marci make her way back to her white BMW, her charm bracelets flickering in the sun. I knew now for certain she wanted to see me. That was her main intention. I knew deep down she had heard about Jack and me. I needed to call him right that second, but I didn't want the girls to know about his marriage to her, or how he found her with two men in his own marital bed just before he divorced her. All of that was his story to tell and I respected his privacy. At least for the moment. I was trying to be good but it was tough—especially with Marci in town.

Just then Coco burst back inside with Jean Pierre right behind him.

"Girl, this is gonna be quite the shindig!" He promised snapping his fingers. "We got this. Carolers, and gorgeous men in fancy tux and tails parking cars. And Honey, we're gonna find us some Victorian carolers to pop in at the very end. Whew, I for one can't even contain my excitement."

I looked at Drew, standing in the background, a *what-can-I-do?-* grin on his face.

"Sounds so fabulous!" I cooed. But all I really wanted was for everybody to go now so I could call Jack and get this Marci thing straightened out. We all said our goodbyes with a hug, and I dashed upstairs to my cell phone. I left Jack a voicemail that I needed to meet him ASAP about something really important. I didn't say what. Just as I was fixin' to rush up stairs, a tiny box hidden behind the big tree on the desk caught my eye. I walked over to get a better look. It had my name on it in dark green letters. A tiny white box for jewelry, I suspected. I opened it up to find a charm. One teensy simple gold charm. It was a dandelion bloom. No card. And I didn't own a charm bracelet. Hmm, I wondered. Who could have left this? It was like a gift from heaven from Granny. She and I had a thing about dandelions being magical—wishes, she'd say. Not weeds.

Jack must be doing this, I thought. I smiled as I clutched the box to my chest and turned back to the stairs. I flew into my large walk-in closet and dressed up—like Marci—though I wasn't totally conscious of it. Cream light wool pants, high heels and a low cut black cashmere sweater. I poofed my hair and slid on red lipstick. Blake introduced me to Mac Rubywoo. It is the perfect 40s red. Perfumed with my pearl dangly earrings and gold bangles and I was ready to go. I wanted to look amazing. Smell amazing. I wanted Jack to choose me, though he already had. My insecurities were flaring after seeing Marci with my own eyes, in the flesh for the first time. What if he knew she was here and didn't tell me? What if she's trying to rekindle something with Jack? *She must be divorced*, I surmised as I locked the back door and headed out to my car, lost in a whirl of thoughts. She is using her maiden name.

All of these thoughts were causing a tornado in my head, swirling around, kicking up dust from my past. That insecure girl, not quite as stunning as everyone else, at least in my own mind, was suddenly visible in my head. I wanted her to leave but she stayed and nagged at me as I started my car. Just as I turned to look out of my back window and put the car in reverse to leave my driveway I caught a glimpse of her. Marci was sitting in her BMW right across the street. She was most definitely waiting—watching for me.

CHAPTER 7

I felt my throat try to close. I gulped and in a moment of insanity, decided to just back out as fast as I could, praying she didn't plan to follow me. I turned the opposite way and glanced up to my rearview window—only to see her making a U-turn in the middle of the street. She was going to follow me—I was now sure—right to Jack. I was suddenly positive this was her plan all along. I wondered what to do. Panic was setting in. The very last thing I wanted was to lead her straight into a reunion with her ex-husband—my Jack. *No way*, I told myself as I felt my inner redneck surface. He's my man now. I don't give a rat's ass if you do look like one of those Hollywood types—the ones that stole my first husband.

I knew that was why I was so sensitive to this. Marci wasn't any ex. She was physically perfect. So all that unsettled stuff I went through with Jason our first couple of years in Hollywood just wrapped its ugly tentacles around me and was trying to strangle me. But those plastic types had nothing on me now. I was the owner of a gorgeous historical inn and was surrounded by other beautiful Belles—who also were part redneck. I wanted to lose her from following me but I had to think fast.

Jack had asked me to meet him at the radio station. He went on the air at 3 o'clock so we could grab some coffee in the break room before show time. I decided to call Blake. I knew if I called Vivi, she'd tell me to slam on brakes and cause her to rear end me. This would be an accident that would be all Marci's fault, which Vivi would love. Blake was a little less reactionary.

"Well, honey, you can always drive over here to my office first. Then we can slip out the back, and jump in my car. She'll think you're inside the law office with me all afternoon. I'll run you over to the station and you can duck inside. Call Abbey and she'll come down and let you in the back way." Blake was a genius.

I drove there and parked right in front along the street. The forecast was calling for freezing rain, after some morning sun. It was so cold that afternoon. Winter wind hit my face as I got out and shut the car door. Winter weather in the Deep South could change on a dime. The sunny day was slipping into the wintry mix faster than it was supposed to and I sure didn't want to get caught out in it. I pulled my large crimson cape up around my shoulders, and flung the end over my left shoulder as I hurried into the little law office, my high heels clicking on the concrete. I parked near DePalma's –the Italian eatery where Jack and I had our first real date several months ago. I noticed it quickly and it warmed my heart as I slipped inside to see Blake.

"Hey honey, Blake's waitin' on you. Come on back," Wanda Jo offered as she stood from her desk and led the way down the narrow hallway. Wanda Jo had been Blake's secretary and legal assistant forever. She was warm and funny. Blake had always loved her and made it known she couldn't do her job or run her practice without her.

"Hey sugar, the big bad wolf on your scent? Get in here and we'll throw her off track," Blake said standing up to give me a hug. "You smell fabulous and look amazing. That Marci's got nothin' on you, honey!" Blake could always make me feel confident. Her self-assurance had just rubbed off on me. And it was exactly what I needed.

"Thanks, I needed that," I said, pulling at my sweater, self-consciously.

"Lets lose her," Blake sassed as she got up from behind her desk. "Com'on, sweetie, I'll just grab my coat and we can make a run for it."

"Yes, ma'am. Right behind you," I answered smiling. We both made our way out to the back parking lot; the sun had already disappeared, grayish purple bloated clouds taking its place. I knew I was in good and very capable hands with Blake. It felt so wonderful and secure having friends around me. I had been strong for far too long. I tried with all my heart to need no one, do it all on my own. But by the time I got home for Daddy's funeral I didn't even realize how broken inside I had become. So tough. Holding everything inside the self-made armor I had built over years and years of being let down, abandoned, and lonely. I could feel that armor coming off now, layer by layer. I was just learning to trust Jack too--until today when Marci showed up on my doorstep at the mansion.

Blake and I left, driving out of the back lot of her law office and circling around the corner to the left of the lot, then around the old bank building where the city clock had stood for decades, one of my favorite relics in Tuscaloosa. Downtown Tuscaloosa was always such a wonderful sight to me but especially at Christmastime. The city streets were decorated; swags of holly and garland with red berries draped the streets from side to side. Wreaths hung in the center of the garland. We drove straight down Greensboro Avenue, past the Bama Theater, where all the beauty pageants of my childhood had been held; Marci never even looked up. She was in an angled space outside DePalma's. She never saw us. Blake was too cool. She and Vivi made the best duo. Vivi was full of wild ideas and never held her tongue and Blake, strong and sensible but still full of adventure. Blake could smartly carry out Vivi's far-fetched ideas. I had lucked out that they included me back into our little Sassy Belle fold. The three of us had created our little club, called The Sassy Belles, when we were in eighth grade. But then my parents moved us to Charleston, and later divorced and I lost all I had held dear—not to mention all my security. Finding them when I came home brought me more joy that I had known since I lost them all those years ago. Having them back, and now Jack too, I had finally regained the life I had loved as a child—and now owning my childhood home that belonged to my Granny was the icing on the cake.

"Now listen to me, Rhonda, if I'm prying or overstepping just say the word," Blake turned to me before I got out. "But I am getting a strong sense that there's more going on here than just a simple ex college girlfriend. I mean you and Jack are obviously very connected…you seem nearly married; a couple in every sense of the word. Marci is nothing to him. Right?"

My tongue suddenly went dry. I wasn't ready to talk about Jack's past, but I so needed some advice. Blake was the most perfect person to get some direction on this. I took a long slow deep breath, and decided to let her in on everything.

"Ok, honey. You don't have to talk. Just know that whenever you need to talk it out, whatever it is, I'm here." Blake reached over and patted my arm as she turned onto 17th street and into the parking lot of WCTR radio. Both of my sisters, Abigail and Annabelle, fraternal twins, worked here. Abby was the Promotions Director and Annie had her own talk show, Saved By The Belle. This was also where Jack had his own sports radio show. My heart began to race as Blake's car rolled to a stop, right next to that beautiful candy apple red mustang. Jack's car. He was right inside. So my questions about Marci were bubbling on the surface. I had so much going on in my head I felt like I was fixin' to pop. I decided to tell Blake.

"Ok, you're right. But none of this can go any further than this car."

"Promise." She smiled reassuringly.

"Jack and Marci were married."

"Oh my Lord. I thought they were just a fling in college—you know cheerleader football star kinda thing."

"No. It did end before they graduated, but then when he played for New England he ran into her. She was there at a game. I'm pretty sure she became some sort of groupie for big football stars. She and Jack got married and within a couple of years things fell apart. He wanted to start a family, she didn't. One day, he came home to find her in bed—with two other men. At the same time."

"Oh, Rhonda!" Blake grabbed her chest. "Well surely he has absolutely no interest in her anymore. That was several years ago now, I'm sure. Jack hasn't played ball in at least a few years. He's been back here working at the radio station since he left the Patriots."

"I know—but why is she here then? Why didn't Jack tell me last night?"

"Only one way to find out. Get in there and get your man. Marci doesn't even matter to him anymore—you'll see. And with the way you look today, honey, he's gonnna want to take you right there in the studio—you'll see. Marci who?" She smiled reassuringly.

I leaned over and hugged her just as the first drops of sleet hit her windshield. "Thanks, honey. What did I ever do without you and Vivi?" I shook my head as I opened the door and stepped out into the frozen droplets of rain. I ran to the back door of the old Brooks mansion that had been saved by Vivi's husband Lewis and was now the home of the The Crimson Tide Radio Network.

I had called Abby and asked her to let me in through the back.

"Get in here, honey." She said as I trotted to the door.

I turned and waved goodbye to Blake as she backed out.

"Thanks, Abby. I really appreciate this."

"Sure, but what the hell is going on?"

I filled her in, even telling her that this Marci woman is Jack's ex.

"And she was trying to follow you here? My God! What is wrong with her? Whatdya think she wants?"

"I don't have the first clue. But I'm fixin' to find out. Jack may not even know she's here." I leaned over and hugged my sister as I turned and went toward Jack's office. "Thanks, Abby. I'll let you know what hits the fan."

I swallowed hard and walked tentatively to the front of the station until I came to Jack's office, just across from the studios. I saw my gorgeous man sitting there at his desk looking over a game roster for the National Championship. I paused for a moment, taking him in. A vision of him just the night before, doing his funny striptease for me, dancing in the shadows of moonlight that flooded in my bedroom at the mansion sifted through my mind. He was so innocent. He had no idea what was fixin' to hit him. I felt a knot grow and tighten in my stomach. I tapped on the door.

CHAPTER 8

"There's my gorgeous girl, get over here," he said standing from behind his desk and removing his little silver glasses. I moved over and hugged him tight, like I might lose him. "You smell delicious," he murmured in my ear. "I love all these little sparkles of ice in your hair. The sun sure didn't last long today." He nuzzled me closer, kissing my neck.

God he smelled good. His navy cashmere sweater was loose and I ran my hands up under it, feeling the warmth of his body against mine.

But he could sense my body was rigid and nervous. "What is it, baby? You seem so anxious."

I pulled back from him and looked into his eyes. Ocean blue with that sparkle I fell in love with when I was only fourteen. My heart beat faster when he held me. My worries about Marci began to melt. I decided to ask him about the charm first.

"Do you recognize this?" I asked with a little grin.

"I can barely see it—let me look. Nope. Why?"

"I found it behind the tree, on the check in desk, just sitting there so I would find it."

"Not from me, baby. Maybe one of your sisters?" Jack pulled me in for another kiss. I dropped the little white gift box back into my purse. I was stalling—I didn't want to get into anything about his ex but I had no choice. I had to get it out.

"Jack, I had a visitor this morning. Even though I had never met her, well, lets just say her reputation precedes her."

"Who?"

"Well," I took a deep breath as my mouth went dry and my stomach churned. I bit my bottom lip, a nervous habit. "Marci showed up at the mansion. Vivi answered the door so she never saw me—at least until I left the inn to come meet you."

"Oh my God, what happened then?"

"Well, she was actually sitting outside across the street from the inn. I saw her watch me get in my car when I went to back out. Then she followed me."

"Oh God. I can't believe it. What did you do?"

"I wanted to confront her, but I decided to act like I never saw her. I guess I needed to prove to myself that she would actually tail me. She must've known instinctively that I was on my way to see you. I mean, Jack—tell me—does she know you live here now? Is she here looking for you?" I swallowed hard again—I wasn't sure I wanted to hear the answers.

"Oh, Rhonda." He paused. "I wanted to tell you last night."

"You mean you knew? You knew that woman was here and you chose not to tell me? How could you even sleep last night? I mean I know you had that piece of my nighty stuck in your mouth but it sure didn't prevent you from talking well enough to tell me she was here."

"Please, just listen," he begged.

"I think I've heard enough. The simple fact that you knew she was here and you didn't tell me. Jack, did you know that she is booked to stay at the Inn this weekend? And in case you've forgotten, this weekend is the big Christmas Gala. Did you know about that?"

He just stared at me. He didn't have to say another word. The silence was heavy. The freezing rain tapping against his office window was deafening in the quiet stagnant room. An eerie light crept through the glass, as the skies outside darkened. The mood had shifted—trust had cracked. I could barely speak. Jack had known Marci was booked in my inn. The day the call came from her, my intern, Josie, had been answering the phones while I had gone shopping for decorations with Vivi.

I had so many questions but my mouth wouldn't move. Like a

video running in my head, scenes of Jason and his Hollywood types flickered like an old super 8 movie. Moments where he promised me things were fine between us; all along he was seeing other women, several at one time. Jack broke the silence.

"Rhonda, listen to me. She found my number and called me late yesterday, just before I saw you. She said she had something I needed to see. She was coming in to see her parents for Christmas, and they told her all about the new inn. She did some research and found out from that article in the paper last month that we were seeing each other. She is just curious. She always has been. She is spontaneous and doesn't think. She just reacts. She told me she wanted to meet you and I told her I'd have to ask you first. But then…"

I cut him off. "But then you decided you wanted to strip for me first. How thoughtful."

"No, I mean yes, I mean, well, you answered the door in that little dark blue slinky thing and you smelled so good—why would I want to break the mood you were in? I was gonna tell you but then that little nighty got stuck in my teeth and well, all I could think of was to get it out. I totally forgot about Marci."

"Really? You're telling me that you knew your ex wife was not only coming to see me to check me out but she was booked in my brand new B&B? Please Jack…I know you can do better." By now I was seething.

Marci had called him. He had actually had a phone call with her. Call me unnaturally jealous but that southern belle in me was quickly being strangled by my inner redneck. In that moment I wanted nothing more than to open up a southern fried can of whoop-ass on that slut. But that was just the redneck talkin'. I sat quietly, all these thoughts swirling in my head—until the words formed and stopped in one place. Jack said something that was actually now stuck, playing again and again as if on a loop in my mind. He said Marci had called him because she needed to show him something. So now I knew she wasn't trying to follow me to Jack this morning. She just wanted to get a good look at me. That was why she dropped by the mansion. I was suddenly so glad that Vivi had answered the door and by the time Marci had gotten a look at me, I was dressed up and on my way out.

"So," I finally spoke up, "Are you seeing her? I mean did y'all make a plan to meet so you can finally see whatever this is she has to show you?"

"No, not yet anyway. Listen to me—I seriously have not even an ounce of interest in whatever she has to show me. Marci is a manipulator. I learned that the hard way. She will spin any situation to make it work for her. I told her I was busy for the next few days with so many holiday events and special broadcasts here I can't even see her for at least a couple of days. That way I would have time to tell you she was here. I know for a fact whatever she has to show me is nothing more than a ploy to find out whatever she can about us. That's all. So no worrying—got it?"

I looked deeply at him. My heart was bruised since he didn't warn me Marci was here. But I believed him. Jack was one of those good to the bone souls. He would never go behind my back with anything, especially another woman—and most especially his slutty ex wife. I inhaled a deep breath and offered a tiny smile.

"Okay, Jack. I believe you. But please, baby-- please make sure I know everything that is happening with her. I need to feel like I'm your ally. I'm strong. I have been through a lot with my own ex. So trust me and include me. Deal?"

"Deal," Jack answered as he reached over and brushed my cheek with his fingertips. He smiled at me sweetly and kissed my lips soft and slow. He was mine. And that was all I needed to know. For the moment.

CHAPTER 9

Safe in my bed, notebooks with never-ending lists scattered about, I felt like things might finally be getting under control. I had the menu created for the evening of the Gala, as well as the morning after for all of the guests staying at the inn. I had hired the Fru Frus as both catering help and decorating help, since now their little business, A Fru Fru Affair, was handling both decorating and food for events. They were fabulous and I was certain everything they did would turn out perfectly. Plus, Vivi was right by their side acting as director and overseer for the entire Gala. Menus were being professionally printed and delivered tomorrow. Everything was right on track. So why did I feel so insecure?

It was about 10pm. I flicked on the TV and snuggled down in my soft bed. Breaking News popped up on the screen. Blonde reporter Dallas Dubois was standing right in front of my inn!

"The brand new Southern Comforts Inn is all poised for its big debut this coming weekend with the much talked about Tuscaloosa Christmas Gala. I'm Dallas Dubois Hollingsworth, and I'll have that story next right here. Stay tuned."

"What?" I actually squealed out loud.

I sprang from my cozy bed and padded hurriedly to the window. Yep. Bright lights and a satellite truck were parked in front of my house and there stood Dallas, microphone in her crimson-gloved hand. I immediately grabbed my cell and called Abby and Annie. Their house was only five minutes from me and I needed help. I knew with both of my sisters in the media business they would be able to answer questions and control the little crowd that was growing rapidly outside. I wasn't nearly as comfortable in front of the cameras as both of them were—with Abby in media promotions and Annie on the air; they were my back-up for just this type of event. I knew the media planned to cover the Gala but this was only Monday night. We had four more days so this was just ridiculous in my opinion.

"Get over here now, please," I begged as I hopped around on one foot trying to pull on my jeans. The TV station is outside."

"Well honey, they don't bite. We'll be there in a jiffy. Just hang on," Annie promised. She was our resident Marilyn Monroe look-alike, her southern voice full of a syrupy drawl that would melt any man. Just then—the doorbell rang. Oh God. "Annie they are ringing the doorbell. Hurry it up. I'm not so sure the definition of 'jiffy' is gonna be fast enough."

The doorbell chimed again.

I threw down my cell on the bed and pulled on that black V-neck I had on earlier. Since I was all ready for bed, I was clean-faced with brushed down hair. Certainly not ready for air. What the hell was Dallas ringing my bell for? I was barefoot, finally in jeans and a sweater, throwing on anything other than my granny gown I had on when I was in bed. I hurried down the stairs. The doorbell was ringing for the third time just as I flung it open.

"What?" I winced, winded as if I had been running from a fire. "I mean, can I help you?"

"Hey there Rhonda! How in the world are you, girl? It has been eons since I saw you—way back in junior high when you were such good friends with Blake and Vivi. I cannot even believe you are right here in the flesh as the owner of this place."

Lord, she was a Chatty Cathy—ya-tata ya-tata. *Please hurry it up Abby. I need y'all to give her whatever she wants so she will just go away.*

"Yes, Dallas, so good seeing you too. I'm so sorry. I was upstairs making my lists for the big event. You coming?" I was trying to make small talk and stall her.

"Oh honey, wouldn't miss this for the whole wide world. It's the media event of the entire season," she chirped. "Every news organization I know of is planning on being here the night of the big event. I mean, girl, you have saved a major Tuscaloosa landmark. Plus now it's fixin' to become a brand new major business here, a draw for fans during football season. I am just so thrilled for you."

"Thanks," I said with a weak smile, my heart racing. I just knew she was gonna ask me for a statement on camera. There was no way in hell I was going on TV looking tired and a mess. No. Freaking. Way. Just then, the headlights of Abby's new cream Mercedes C-class bounced off my eyes. Abby and Annie jumped out, both of them dressed to the nines, and quickly made their way up the sidewalk to the porch—where I was trapped in an endless babbling match with the mouth of the south.

"Hey y'all just in time. Y'all both know Dallas." I did the informal introductions then tried to disappear. It didn't work.

"Rhonda, we need to get a quick statement from you. We'll be back on live in thirty seconds."

"Uhm, no, I actually have two spokespeople right here who can answer any questions you might have about the Gala. I'm not really prepared...."

"And we're live in five, four..." Dallas' cameraman began. Dallas positioned her earpiece then shoved the mic right under my nose. My hair was a mess, I had my reading glasses sitting at the bottom of my nose, bare feet, no bra—it just couldn't get much worse. Oh wait. I suddenly recalled when it actually *was* worse. The night I came face to face with Jack for the first time since we were teenagers and I had mashed potatoes and butter dripping from my head. The lights were searing in eyes, the microphone and Dallas' huge blonde hair-do in my face. *Speak!* I told myself. I knew I had to.

"Well, I have to say, I'm excited about this weekend's Gala. Please excuse my awful appearance. I'm working hard to make this an evening Tuscaloosa won't ever forget." I smiled a frozen dear-in-the-headlights grin hoping there would be no more questions. I blew a stray hair from my eyes, and kept grinning. Just then my big yellow cat, Miss Priss sprinted from between my legs and ran out into the night. I was so blinded by the camera lights I couldn't see anything but pitch black darkness.

"Oh no!" I squelched. "Miss Priss!" Instinctively, I dove off the porch, tripped down the porch stairs, my bare foot tangling in all of the TV cables.

"Oh my Lord!" Dallas yelped as her TV mic flew out of her hand and dragged along the front yard, wrapped around my ankle.

"I'm on live TV right now, come back here," Dallas shrieked as she chased after me, her cameraman running behind her. Abby and Annie bringing up the rear. All of it caught on live television, as a line of women, dressed in high heels pranced across my yard, chasing me, tangled in cables.

"Daniel, are you getting this?" Dallas panted over her shoulder to her videographer. She was huffing and puffing as she ran in her winter white coat and heels across the grass. "This is spectacular. It could get me an Emmy."

"Here Miss Priss, here kitty kitty," I cajoled as I kept running till I suddenly lost my balance, the cable went taught, yanking me straight back and down I went. Face first.

"Somebody grab Miss Priss," I blurted as I went down.

"I got her." I heard a woman's voice say. But it sure didn't sound like the sing- songy southern drawl of Dallas' off air tone. My face was covered in mud from the wet freezing rain of the afternoon, blades of dead grass and muck hung from my nostrils. My glasses askew, now propped sideways on my face. Spread eagle face down, a blanket of total embarrassment covered me. My TV debut. I opened my eyes and spit out some mud when I saw the shoes. The crimson suede pumps.

"Nice little kitty. Is this what you're chasing?" She bubbled.

I peered upwards, wiping grass from my nose, to see, standing in my yard, holding my fat orange cat, none other than Marci Miller.

CHAPTER 10

"Hi," I said standing up. I brushed off my jeans and swallowed hard, tasting dirt. My bare feet were no match for her five foot nine inch frame, especially since she was in high heels. She towered over me. It was a sight and oh so lovely. Ahem. NOT! I felt suddenly nauseous. I decided to play dumb.

"Thanks so much, I'll take her now," I said, reaching for Miss Priss. "And you are?"

"I'm Marci Miller. I came by this morning so I could get a look at the new refurbished mansion. But I couldn't get inside. Some redhead said it was still a private residence till Friday."

"Oh, well Mrs. McFadden Heart *is* one of the owners and she is absolutely correct; it is still a private residence. Why did you need to get in?"

"Oh no big reason. I just wanted to see it all before everyone is here for the Gala."

"Oh, well I am so sorry for the inconvenience, but you'll have to wait like everyone else." I smiled, Miss Priss wriggling under my arm. "Thanks for helping me with my cat." Just then Abby, Annie and Dallas arrived at the scene. My poor black cashmere V-neck muddy and damp. My hair stringy, wet grass hanging down, and here was Dallas, light back in my eyes, her mic right back in my face. *Lord, can I please get a break here?*

"I need to get my cat back inside so if you have any further questions please direct those to my sisters who are also co-owners of the inn. Thanks so much for coming, see y'all Saturday." With that I turned toward the mansion, my bare feet squishing into the muddy earth. I had put on an air of confidence. I walked as fast as I could, cooing at Miss Priss, like I was calm and collected. I walked at a clip so no one would be close enough to detect the truth.

Then I felt the sting in my eyes. Tears formed and spilled down my damp cheeks, as I played the role. I glanced over my shoulder just as Marci slammed her car door. Dallas and her cameraman made their way back to the news truck, Daniel trying to wrap the cables I had dragged across the yard. Abby and Annie were on their way to catch up with me. Once I was safely inside my house, I put Miss Priss down onto the hardwood floor, rubbing her back as I let the frustration and exhaustion flow. I sat down on the bottom step near the still bare oversized tree, and rubbed my eyes, dirt under my nails, just as my sisters made their way inside and closed the door.

"I just can't do this anymore," I blubbered, feeling defeated. I was so tired. I had just gone through a major life change, moving home, saving the mansion, my childhood home. Granny Cartwright had been my rock and this place was hers. I owed this to her. I sold my business in LA to my assistants and came home to stay. It had been a lot in such a short amount of time. And now, back with Jack, the very first boyfriend I ever had, surrounded by my old best friends and safe in the bosom of my family—now I find myself with a humungous event I'm not really sure I can pull off—especially with Jack's ex wife showing up in every corner. She jumps out at me like a ghost, lurking in the darkness and following me. I was fixin' to have a hissy fit. I felt it comin' on like a freight train.

"Oh honey, c'mere," Annie said as she scooched in next to me on the staircase. "I know you're just exhausted. It's understandable." She put her arm around me and I laid my head over on her shoulder. "No y'all don't understand. There's more to it," I mumbled as I choked.

"I have figured that much out. I mean just who was that woman all dressed in winter white holding Miss Priss? She looked familiar but since it was dark, I wasn't sure," Abby questioned.

"If I didn't know better I would totally swear that was Marci Miller. She was Miss Tuscaloosa the year before me. She hasn't aged a bit. Was that her?" Annie was stroking my still muddy damp hair.

"The one and only," I affirmed as I began to cry harder, literally boo-hooing out loud.

"Why in the world would she make you cry, sugar? I know she's still so pretty but seriously, you're a cutie-pie too."

Loud sobs now. I couldn't take it. Here comes the afore noted hissy fit.

"Y'all have no earthly idea what I have been through today! Yes, I know that was Marci Miller!" I stood up and faced them. "I also know just how fabulous looking that stinking slut is. But let me tell you one thing," I was using my high-pitched hissy fittin' voice, she's a bitch, I tell you!"

"Honey, listen to yourself. You don't even know her," Abby reassured. "Calm down. What did she want? Why was she even here?"

"I don't have to know her! I know what she did. All day long everywhere I went, there she was, following me like I was a dog in heat. All she wanted to do was gawk at me. Well, now she got her wish didn't she—she saw me alright, in all this wet muddy glory. I'm a disaster…" I started crying harder, with my shoulders bouncing up and down.

"Why would she follow you? Why is she interested in you at all? I mean, not that you're not highly interesting, sweetie, but I think you may have this all wrong." Abby was trying her best to surmise the motivation but she had no idea.

"I do not have anything wrong! Marci wanted to get a look at me. She was curious about me."

"Okay, I give. If this is a guessing game, I'm out." Abby threw her hands up.

"Wait, let me guess," Annie chirped. "I'm still playing." She was so childlike—she couldn't help it.

"For God's sake, Annie, this isn't like Charades! Tell us what the hell is going on!" Abby was pushing.

I cried even harder and staring at both of them through the squalls of an infant I threw it out in the open. "Marci is Jack's ex."

"Oh, I do remember they dated in college," Annie popped.

"Yeah, so what if she and Jack dated in college. Hell you were even married, Rhonda," Abby reasoned.

"Well so was Jack. To Marci. Until he arrived home early one afternoon to find her in bed with two men. Two men at the same time. So yes, she is a slut and a bitch too with a cherry on top!"

"Oh my God!" Annie and Abby said simultaneously.

"Yes, See? I told you. And this is how I meet her finally? She just kept popping up out of nowhere all day long. I kept acting like I didn't see her."

"So what? I mean, really who even cares? Jack would never take her back. So she saw you and you were a mess. You are the one who has Jack. And nothing's gonna change that."

"Yeah, honey. So Marci can go to hell," Annie quipped.

"No, she can't. Not unless this is hell." I said.

"Huh?" Annie asked.

"She's booked here in one of the rooms as a guest the night of the Christmas Gala."

"What in the world is she after?" Abby wondered out loud.

"She said she had something to show Jack but he thinks she's just manipulating him for some one-on-one time. So won't that be just the perfect little soiree? With the media all over me like bees makin' honey, I'm already gonna be a nervous wreck the night of the Gala. But no, that won't be enough pressure. I have to watch Marci all night long. She'll surely be after Jack the whole evening for a little private chat with him. What could she want? What could she have to show him?"

All of us were silent as that last question hung in the air. I could hear all of us breathing in the front hall. My stomach twisted. Just breath—in silence.

"You don't think...?" Abby looked at me with a worried stare not finishing her sentence.

"Oh no," Annie uttered shaking her head. "Surely not."

"Y'all aren't thinking what I'm thinking are you? Please say you're not."

"What, Rhonda? What are you thinking? Just say it."

"That maybe Marci has a child. And it's Jack's?"

CHAPTER 11

Those words hung in the air, a deadly silence swirling between the three of us. No one spoke another word. My stomach clenched as the words tumbled from my mouth. Then finally, Abby broke the stillness.

"There's no way I believe that. Marci is an opportunist. She and Jack have been divorced for at least two years. She would never have kept the child a secret—she could use the poor little thing to have control over Jack. Right? It just can't be a child."

"No I don't think so either," Annie added. "I agree with Abby. Marci's a control freak. I knew her in pageants and she is very high-strung. It doesn't fit her personality at all to hide a child. She would have been controlling Jack and stealing his money all this time. So we need to think of what else it could be."

"I think she's just up to her old tricks—trying to figure out how she can get Jack's attention and compete with you. Why don't we call it a night? Tomorrow's gonna be a long day," Abby suggested, helping me up the stairs. Annie got on the other side of me and the three of us headed up the curved staircase to my oversized master suite.

Abby and Annie stayed with me till I was ready for bed. Talking, trying to keep my mind off things, they laughed but it all sounded a little like a far-away echo to me…I was lost in a trance, seeing Jack so upset earlier today, images of a child he may not know about, Marci, holding my cat and me covered in grass and mud—with no make-up.

And it was all caught on tape—no, live TV. Great!

"Alrighty, honey—now get some sleep. We'll check in tomorrow." Annie leaned down and kissed my forehead. She was the soft sweet one. Abby was more of a realist. Even though she was younger than me, she was very motherly—Annie and I both leaned on her. Her strength and intelligence were the backbone of the three of us. Ever since Mother and Daddy's divorce, Abby held us together. I was the dreamer, Annie the romantic, Abby, the practical, logical sister who could lead the way.

"Now listen, I know you, Rhonda, you'll worry all night long, look like hell warmed over tomorrow and barely get a thing done. Do not let your imagination run away with you," Abby leaned over and gave me a squeeze. "You'll picture the kid looking just like Jack and have Marci using him to get Jack back into her life—honey it's not real. I am positive there is no hidden baby. Now get some rest and we'll see you tomorrow."

They both smiled, Annie blowing a kiss, as they left the room and descended the stairs. I heard the click of the lock as they left the inn. Since they both had bought an interest in it, everyone had a key. Blake and Vivi were more active as part owners but we all owned a piece of the place. That was such a comfort. At least I knew that no matter what, my girls always had my back. I never had that before.

It was nearly midnight as I tried to snuggle down into my warm duvet. The sounds of the winter's night crept in, sleet tapping on my frosty window, the winds bending the bare tree branches. I wanted to call Jack—my heart screaming at me to grab my cell and hit his number. But the future suddenly felt uncertain. I felt like I knew him with my whole heart, that gut-wrenching tug to love him, trust him...his kisses held promises and emotions of forever. I knew he was mine.

So why in the hell did I toss and turn all night long?

* * *

Morning came too early, awakened by my ringing cell. I rolled over dragging the white sheets with me still tucked under my chin.

"Hello," I muttered.

"Girl, you are totally not gonna believe this! Wake up, honey and look out your window." Coco was giddy with excitement. I dragged myself out from under the covers leaving the warmth behind and stumbled over to the window.

"Oh my God!" I yelled even though I was in the house alone. I blinked my eyes twice in hopes what I saw might be a bad dream. But no. There stood Coco, his arms flailing about like he was trying to flag a car at Talladega. He was dressed in bright red skinny jeans and a black sweater, a chevron print green and white scarf doubled around his neck. He was waving like a wild fool with a humungous grin on his face, totally surrounded by at least ten little people, all of the dressed up like Santa's elves. It looked like a freaking circus had hit the mansion. My mouth wouldn't close. I threw open the window so I could hear what Coco was yelling and stuck my head out into the freezing morning air.

"Dontcha just love me? I got us some real live elves, honey!"

"I see," I shouted back down to him. Love wasn't exactly what I was feeling. "I'll be right there." I threw on some black leggings and a long cream sweater along with my Ugg boots and headed downstairs at a clip and straight out to the front yard, just as a little person turned a cartwheel and hit me right across my left boob.

"Ouch!" I yelped, grabbing my breast.

"Oh girl, I am so sorry," Coco blurted as he trotted across the yard. "Y'all calm it down right this minute," he demanded with his hands on his hips. They all stopped running around my yard, performing acrobatic tricks, just as he punctuated the moment with a singular snap over his head.

"Coco, I am so…uhm, surprised," I managed. "It is so early and really, this is just, uhm…something."

"They are so fab, aren't they? Okay, tell me I'm amaz—ing," he sang. "I totally couldn't believe it but I found me an agency in Hotlanta and they sent them all over, even put 'em up in a hotel for the week so we can get an act together."

"Are they gonna preform?"

"Well, of course they are! They have to sing! 'We Are Santa's

Elves'...you know that's a good song for them. We have to get them a routine and get'em ready to go. It's almost show time, sugar!"

I knew it was too late to do anything. I wanted an elegant affair. That was the goal. Classy, uptown, elegance. For the life of me I couldn't figure out how those cartwheel-turning pixies were gonna mix with my whole theme of grandeur and sophistication. But at this point, I just decided to go with it. I had too much left to do. It was Tuesday and by Friday night my first guests would be arriving. Saturday night was to be posh and luxurious. And it would be. Or else. Even with Santa's little acrobats running crazy.

"Well, sweetie, you have sure topped yourself. Have you told Vivi?" I asked him, knowing I would need back-up if the elves got out of control.

"Nope. I haven't even told Jean-Pierre. Won't they be so surprised?

"Uhm yes, just ecstatic," I shot back. "Okay, well, y'all thanks so much for coming. I gotta get back inside and get to work. But Coco, I just can't wait to see the routine you have in mind. Remember, the theme is elegance and glamour. Keep it simple and classy, okay?" I knew that was like telling Lady GaGa to wear sensible shoes. I smiled as I hugged Coco and turned to head back inside.

"Come on y'all. Back to the hotel. We got a big number to learn. Oh! I am so excited! I have always dreamed of being a choreographer," I heard Coco exclaim as I headed up the porch steps.

God help me was all I could think.

I closed the door and heard my cell ringing upstairs.

"Hello," I managed, out of breath by the time I picked it up.

"Well you're up early. You sound like you been training." It was Jack. His sexy earthy morning tones sent a shiver of heat up my back. Even though I had been pretty mad at him yesterday, he wasn't the type you could stay mad at for long.

"Yes, I guess my secrets out now. I joined a club—*How to open the perfect can of whoop-ass on his ex.* The first class was actually late last night."

"Oh, Rhonda. Did Marci come back?"

"Why yes, she most certainly did," I mocked with my sweetest southern accent. "That Marci is so sweet too. She caught my cat for me. Isn't she just wonderful?" I asked, sarcasm dripping from my tongue.

"Do I detect a note of irritation?"

"Nope, it wasn't just a note, it was pretty much a symphony of *hissy fit.*"

"Glad I missed that concert," he said clearing his throat. "How are you this morning? Really. All kidding aside."

I wanted to tell him how I was not really okay. Especially after last night and meeting Marci face to shoe in my front yard. How her even being in town made me antsy. And especially how Marci staying at my inn during the Gala had me in knots. But I decided to play it cool. I felt in my gut that I knew Jack. He was mine. I just kept telling myself that over and over. Eventually I'd believe myself—I hoped.

"I'm okay. I have a list a mile long to get done before the Gala so I was just fixin to hop in the shower and get the day goin'. How are you? Tooth all better now?" I asked trying to be open to him.

"The doctor had quite a laugh," he answered with a hint of awkwardness. "I wanted to tell you yesterday but the whole Marci thing came up. He gave me the piece of your silk nighty to keep. I have it in my wallet. Your slinky little gown stuck in my teeth—he said he had never seen that one before." Jack was trying to be light. I knew he was worried that I was still upset. And truth be told, I was a little wary. He knew his ex was in town and he didn't tell me right away. But in order to move past all this, and get on with the Gala, I had to let it go and give him the benefit of the doubt.

"I'm glad you have the little remembrance," I said, softening my voice so he would know things were okay.

"Wanna pick up where we left off? I know life is crazy this week for you but all the more reason you'll need help relaxin'. I think I can be of service," he teased.

"Oh you do, do you? Can you tell me about the services you offer?" I chided.

"Well, massages are my specialty. Relaxing tense muscles, you know, pretty much all over. I'm pretty good if I do say so myself. So whadya think? Would you like to book a time with me today?"

"Yes, I think I would. I better be your only customer too. I am pretty sure I'd like to go ahead and book you solid," I played, a giggle caught in the back of my throat.

"Oh, that'll be fine—for how long?" He asked.

"Oh, let me think—how about for the next several months? I cooed.

"I have a better idea," he broke in. "How about forever?" Jack was smooth, but so genuine.

I knew I was right. All of the last twenty-four hours I had been telling myself to relax. He was mine. I had nothing to worry about— Marci or no Marci. I inhaled a deep breath and let it out. "I think I can swing that," I finally agreed.

"Perfect, is now too early?" He jumped in.

"Don't you have a second job, some radio thing," I teased.

"It doesn't start for hours, I think I can fit you in this morning? How about thirty minutes from now?"

"Oh, you make house calls?"

"They're my specialty."

I checked the vintage sage green clock on my bedside table. 8 AM. It was perfect. I had an appointment with Drew at 11:30 that morning. Then I was meeting Blake and Vivi for lunch. The Fru Frus were coming to finish the indoor Christmas decorations at two. Full day. But the most important thing to me was Jack. I wanted him to know we were okay. I needed to see him too.

Had breakfast yet, he asked.

"No, not yet. Are you going to be my breakfast?"

"I'll be your dessert. You're gonna need sustenance, promise. I'll run by The Waysider and grab some breakfast and see you in half an hour."

"Oh, Gosh, that sounds awesome. I'm starved."

The Waysider was a Tuscaloosa mainstay and a huge tradition. I had missed this place so much when I was in L.A. Their biscuits and red-eye gravy was out of this world, and every famous person visiting Tuscaloosa dropped by there for breakfast. It was just down on Greensboro Avenue, so it wouldn't take Jack anytime to grab us the delicacies known nowhere else but at the Waysider. Famed football coach bear Bryant literally hung out there and his own table the whole time I was growing up here. I didn't know which I was more excited about, those biscuits or Jack!

I felt my heart begin to race though and my body warmed at the thought of my sweet man. It was early morning but maybe he was the type of guy that was really into mornings. Hell I was into anytime fun with him. I was in love with him. I think that was the very first time I admitted this to myself. I knew for a long time that I loved him. But to be *in* love with him was somehow different. It was unconditional. Even with Marci in town, even though he didn't tell me that, I still would melt when I thought of him. He had me. This was the first time I had felt this way about anyone. It was a forever kind of love. It pulsed through me and excited me. I knew at that second that no matter what Miss Marci Miller had to show Jack, it didn't matter. Jack and I were together. Together—like one. I smiled to myself.

Surely no one would bother us this early. *Finally*, I thought to myself as I turned on the shower, *some uninterrupted time with my Jack.*

CHAPTER 12

I had showered and put on a little make-up, some sexy pink lip-gloss and another silky nighty—this one a tad more fun, lacy with white silk. Very feminine. I tied a ribbon through my hair, letting one of the ends stream down over my shoulder. I sent Jack a text, *Left the front door unlocked, come find me.*

I made my way down to the kitchen and sat in the banquette. I knew he'd run up the stairs the minute he got to the mansion. I sat down on the soft cotton seat, bare feet, one shoulder exposed as my cream silk matching robe draped off my right shoulder. I had lit the fireplaces and some cinnamon scented candles. The house smelled of Christmas and was warm and inviting. I heard the door handle click open then close softly. Jack made his way up the stairs, calling out, "Ma'am—your appointment. Your massage therapist is here. Breakfast is served."

I giggled as I heard him skip back down the stairs, calling out again. This time he heard my snicker and arrived at the door of the kitchen. He leaned on the doorway, his left arm above his head, looking at me with a gleam in his eyes, and a cockeyed grin across his lips.

"You look good enough to eat," he murmured in his deepest slowest voice, a lilt of southern harmony rolled across his tongue. I wanted to devour him. "So is this where you'd like me to perform my magic? I think the island over there just might be the perfect spot—for me to find your perfect spot."

"I'm game," I teased. "Just leave the breakfast on the table."

Jack sauntered over, removing his glasses and leaving them on the table along with those mouth-watering biscuits.

He slid his arms around the small of my back, pulling me snuggly into his chest.

Then I felt a lump in his coat. I smiled as Jack pulled out a gift, wrapped in bright red paper with a huge white bow.

"I owed you something," he teased and kissed my neck. "Open it."

I sat down in the chair at the end of the banquette, and ripped into the little box. The beautiful white box, with *Belk's* written on the outside made me wonder—then smile. I pulled the tape apart and the top off, separated the pink tissue paper to reveal a lacy cream colored silk nighty, spaghetti straps and all. "Oh, Jack. This is so gorgeous. I love it! It's perfect." I jumped up and hugged him, his face still cool from the chill in the outside air.

"Wanna see me in it?"

"Right here?"

"Well you were fixin' to give me a massage, so I do believe this is perfect for that occasion," I purred.

I grabbed the negligee, and headed into the powder room just off the kitchen to change. I came out to find Jack, waiting on me with no shirt, his gorgeous flat chest, heaving deep excited breaths, his tight blue jeans sexy and taut at the center.

"I work better without my shirt," he affirmed softly. "Don't mind do ya?" He removed his shirt and his white tee-shirt beneath it, reveling tanned hard muscles, his chest so hard and smooth I leaned in to touch it—I was losing control.

"No, ma'am. I am here all for you," he said as he scooped me from the end of the banquette seat and carried me cradled in his arms to the kitchen island and lied me back. Full sun streamed in through the windows. Making love in bright sunlight was something I had never done before. It heightened my senses.

"Relax," he leaned down and whispered to me. "I work well using, lets say, unconventional massage oils. Be right back." Jack turned to the fridge as I watched him grab the chocolate sauce, whip cream, and some sea-salted caramel sauce, along with some eggnog. My heart raced as my body heated. I felt a rush of warmth flare as a bead of perspiration rolled around my breast. Jack turned to me.

"My mouth works as well as my hands," he promised. He leaned down and kissed my neck, his tongue rolling around under my jaw.

I reached to touch his glorious chest, his hand grasping my wrist midway. "No, no. I am working here. No interruptions or distractions please," he ordered smiling.

I knew it was going to be his pleasure to drive me to the brink. He continued. He moved and began at my feet, working his magic with both his hands. Up my legs, to my inner thighs, his lips doing more work than his fingers. I let him have me. He stopped to spread whip cream onto my skin, the cool smooth essence followed by the warmth of his lips, his mouth, his tongue. I was delirious.

Just then a rapid banging began on the back door. "Drew's probably early," I said with a pout.

The banging picked up again with intense urgency. "I'm comin' I'm comin' Drew. Hang on!"

Jack smiled at the irony of my last words. I flung my bare thighs from the center island and dangled my feet till I reached the hardwood floor, sliding off. I stopped long enough to blow Jack a kiss. "Hold that thought," I said with a wink. I saw Jack scamper around the corner to the dining room to wait for me to signal it was all clear. Drew was to be working outside so I could answer him, and then send him off to get going on the yard decorations. Then Jack and I could pick up right where we left off.

Without even thinking, I grabbed the doorknob and opened the backdoor, the yellow toile curtains blocking my view, only to see Marci standing on my back steps.

"Good morning," she chirped. "I'm here to see Jack."

I gulped. I was taken aback, seeing her standing in front of me looking tasteful and perfect. It infuriated me. I wanted to push her off the back steps. Instead, I lied. "Jack's not here," I grinned, trying hard to block her from seeing Jack, keeping the door just cracked enough for her to notice my bare feet.

"Oh? Well, his car is right out front," Marci pushed, motioning with her hand to the front drive.

Jack stepped toward me, then stopped midway dead in his tracks, staring at Marci. He was face to face with his ex, for the first time in years. He wanted this to end—for her to leave me alone. So he appeared from the other room to help me get rid of her. He was such a man.

I inhaled a deep breath and smirked at him. "Oh, honey, I didn't hear you come in. This woman is looking for you."

"Hello Jack. Is this your attire for visiting friends on a cold winter morning? And, Rhonda, is this how you always answer the door? Are you sure it's an inn you're running here? Looks more like a brothel."

"What can I help you with, Marci? I think I told you it would be next week before I could talk. Are you following me now? I know you've been following Rhonda," Jack asserted as he entered the kitchen fully.

"Oh no. Not following. Just trying to talk to you. I need to give you these." She pulled a large manila envelope from her oversized Hermes and handed it to Jack.

"What's this?"

"Just take a look at it and tell me what you'd like to do."

Jack opened the envelope. He sifted through the paper-clipped stack of papers. "These are our divorce papers," he looked up, positioning his glasses to a better fit on his nose.

"I know what they are," Marci snapped. You never signed them."

CHAPTER 13

I stood there dumbfounded. The silence so thick it was suffocating me. The freezing air swirled inside the still open back door, Jack stood shirtless with his mouth formed in a perfect "O".

"Jack? Are you okay? Did you have any idea about this?" I finally broke the silence. Jack didn't speak. He just kept sifting through the pages. He seemed to totally forget he was barely dressed.

"Well, thank you for coming. We'll get back to you." I tried to take the lead and get rid of her.

"Just a damn minute. I have come a long way, Jack. You're now having a full on affair with this woman. You are still married to me. Now if you want this over and done with just sign the papers. Or I can always go to the media and let them know we are still married. Won't that be a boost to your new broadcast career, Jack? Oh, and I'm quite certain it will be fabulous for the big Christmas Gala this weekend. You decide."

"No! *You* wait a damn minute. What is this? I caught you in bed, with two of my teammates. You were the one having an affair. You made me look like a fool. I don't know what this is, but I know I signed papers. These aren't even real." He flung them down on the counter.

"Please kindly leave my home, Marci. And By the way—thanks for catching my cat. Have a good day." I slammed the back door in her face, my yellow curtains flying.

I turned and looked at Jack. He was a wreck. My heart was racing and my throat was clenched, a lump blocking my words.

"I swear, baby. I swear. I *know* I'm divorced. She signed before me but I'm sure I signed these too. She just wants back at me. In the end, before I left Boston, she was the one that looked like a fool. The affair was all over the media. I just snuck out of town as quick as I could."

I reached up and stroked his dark sandy hair, still mussed from my fingers tangling in it just moments ago. I loved this man. He was hurting and angry. I wanted to kick that Marci's ass for him. "Could there be any way at all? Any way you might not be divorced?"

"No way. I am a hundred percent sure I signed. Plus, look at this! Okay. I see it now. I see what she's doing." Jack pointed to a section within the pages he held. "Read this." He said sliding the pages to me.

I read the paper, my hands shaking as I digested what was happening. "No," I cried, "She can't can she?"

"I sure as hell don't think so. This place is ours. I went in with you on your half. You will still have your half if she decides to try to take it all. She can only get part of mine. But listen to me, Rhonda. This is fake. I know it is. I know I already signed."

I started to tear up. The shaking grew until I could barely stand. When all of us decided to own shares in the Southern Comforts Inn, Blake and Vivi, Annie and Abby all split half of the entire property between the four of them, and all the assets and future income would be divided among them. So each of them evenly split fifty percent. Jack wanted to be part of it all in an even bigger way. Not only because it was mine and it would help keep me here instead of moving back to L.A., but also because he loved being able to give back to Tuscaloosa. The city had been so good to him during his college years.

What was in the *new* divorce decree that Marci showed to Jack said she would attain half of all of his assets, things he had attained in their marriage but also everything he would build as business assets in the future. She claimed that she helped him build his name into national notoriety when they were married. So any way that he would make money in the future, she wanted half. That meant she would take what he had and divide it and now Marci would be a partner—

with the rest of us—in my new inn! If Jack refused to give up his half, she had a legal right to sue him for all of it, according to this divorce decree.

So the way it looked was, if Jack wanted to fight her, he wouldn't sign, which meant he was still married. If he signed to be legally divorced, I would lose part of the inn to Marci. I stated bawling like a baby. I felt trapped. With the Gala just days away, we had to get this solved. I knew there was no way I could share anything with Marci. But we only had a few days and I knew she would keep her promise and go to the media, spreading lies that Jack is still married and the owner of the inn, me, was now in some affair. She was blackmailing Jack. Mad tears streamed down my cheeks.

"We're stuck with her. You have to sign. Don't you, Jack? You need to get away from this before she ruins us both.

"No. What I need is an attorney."

"Great, well we have one as an owner." Suddenly I felt a tiny tinge of hope. Blake could fix this. She had too. "I'll get her over here right now," I said looking for my cell. "And from what I remember this kind of law is her specialty."

I called Blake and filled her in. " Don't worry honey, I'm on the way. See y'all in two minutes!"

"Okay, baby, she's on the way. She'll figure this out," Jack promised, trying to console me.

"Oh my Lord!" I stopped and glanced at the kitchen clock. "Drew will be here any second. Go put some clothes on and look like you just dropped by. No one needs to think anything happened here. I don't need even one more scandal—not ever. I have had a lifetime of scandals and I am getting tired. Okay, go." I hugged him tightly, holding him for more than just a moment. I pulled back to look at him.

"Rhonda, nothing in this world is gonna make this go away," he pressed. "Never doubt that. I love you and Marci means nothing to me. Look at me a minute."

He slid his fingertips under my jaw and brushed my lips with his thumb as he gazed down into my eyes. "I have never loved anyone like I love you. We are one as far as I'm concerned. That was the whole reason I wanted to buy into this place. I wanted to have something with you. I am a part of you and you are part of me. Please don't cry." He brushed away a tear as it crept down my cheek.

"Blake will fix this," he continued. "I know I have already signed for divorce anyway so none of this is even real. I'm all yours—but even better, you're mine." He took my wrist and placed my hand on his bare chest. "Feel that?" he asked as he pulled my hand directly over his heartbeat. "That is my heart...but you are what makes it beat. Every minute of every day I thank God I found you again. So please know this is a tiny bump and it will be all over in a matter of days." He leaned in and pressed his warm lips to mine. Then he turned and hurried up the stairs to get the rest of his clothes.

I went into the powder room off the kitchen and turned on the water. I looked at myself—a total disaster. I reached for some make-up remover in the cabinet and dampened a cotton pad and wiped my face clean as if I was wiping away the nightmare that had just unfolded at my back door. Marci was sneaky. She purposely decided to use the back porch instead of the front. She knew I wouldn't answer if I saw her. She had to have scoped out my house, watched me at some point. Followed Jack here this morning—who knows? All I knew for sure was that she was an opportunist and a manipulator. I also knew I didn't want anyone knowing a thing. Marci's threat to go to the media had me worried—I had the big event coming and needed good press. Plus I didn't want Jack's name smeared all over the place. She would show the unsigned divorce decree and swear he was cheating on her with me. Oh! I hated that awful heifer. I thought of my girls, my sassy sisters. I knew I had them behind me. Couple that with Jack and my sisters, and even old Drew if I needed him and I knew I had a posse from heaven. Nothing and no one, not even Miss Marci Miller could break the barrier of my new little family.

I suddenly felt stronger. I grabbed some lip-gloss from an old make-up bag and slid it on, powdered my face and rinsed with some mouthwash. I smiled at myself. Jack was right. We would make it through this.

I dare that bitchy woman to try to steal my house form me, I thought. And I double dare her to try to hurt my man.

Now that's the Christmas spirit.

I smiled at myself and shut the medicine cabinet and stepped out to wait for Blake. That Marci had no idea what she was fixin' to get hit with—Hurricane Sassy Belles.

CHAPTER 14

Drew knocked on the back door just as I was finishing up I looked fresh and ready for my day. Not like I had just had the wind knocked outta me. Not like I had *almost* just had the best love-making escapade of my entire life just an hour ago. No. I looked rested and raring to hit the day running.

"Hey Drew. So happy to see you," I announced offering him a hug.

He pulled back and peered into my still red eyes.

"Okay, spill it," he demanded.

"What?" I tried to look really confused.

"Come on. I know that face pretty well by now. I sure know that look like everything just went to hell in a bolt of flames. Tell me. I mean if I'm not intruding."

Oh Drew, Okay." Just then Blake walked up the back steps, her leather briefcase in hand.

"Oh Lordy, somethin's up. I knew it. I could jes feel it deep in my bones. I'm sorry if it's none of my business but you know, Rhonda, I ain't got no kids of my own living 'round here no more—you're like a daughter to me. So I wanna help if I can. If your feelin' bad, well, then I'm gonna feel bad too." He looked so sympathetically at me, his eyes sincere and genuine.

"Oh Drew, I love you. Come on in and sit down. Blake is here to talk about it all and you can jump in whenever you feel like it—okay Blake?"

"I'm fine with that. Drew is family now. Hell he's been here so long, he belongs here with the rest of us." She sat down at the banquette on the outside chair at the end. I got us all some hot coffee and put the cups down in front of them. I sat a plate full of raisin muffins in the center of the table. The coffee was hot and the steam fogged the cold kitchen window over the little nook. I filled them both in with all the details just as Jack came bounding down the stairs and joined us. He was buttoning the cuff of his shirt as he scooched in next to me.

"What'd I miss?" He asked anxiously.

"Well, I was just saying to Rhonda, all of this is easy enough to check out. Most divorces are a matter of public record. I can file to have the records transferred here in about twenty-four hours. As for all the hoopla about her taking Jack's stake in this property, she would have to prove that he was able to attain his share just because he was a former football star."

"That had nothing to do with this deal what-so-ever," Jack interrupted. "I wanted to help Rhonda. This was my own money. I could do whatever I wanted with it."

"That is all true so she is just posturing. It's all just Marci throwing out threats. What I need to do right now is get back and file for the original records. Jack follow me and when we get back to my office you can give me the particulars." Blake slid her chair back across the floor and stood up. She was lovely, pulled together in a winter-white sweater, a long stand of pearls and black wool pants. I admired her so. I always had. Smart and beautiful, and a backbone made of steal. She was what you'd call the real deal, a sassy belle and a steel magnolia wrapped in one.

"Drew you have certainly been quiet. What do ya think about all this?" Blake made small talk as she gathered her pens and notebooks and stuffed them into her Louie Vuitton bag.

"All I know is that if someone hurts my girl here, they gonna have to deal with me too. And I got me a bunch of old redneck cousins outta work if ya know whatta mean."

"No. What do you mean, Drew?" Jack looked curious as a sly little grin crept across his face.

"Well, Miss Miller may find her tire has gone flat on her. That orta stop her from follerin' y'all. Or, she might even find her porch covered in some slick oil. She could fall and hurt somethin'. That'd be such a shame."

"Drew, I'm gonna pretend I didn't hear any of that," Blake smirked.

"Me too, but I like it," I said winking at him.

"Rhonda, we still on for a late lunch? Vivi is planning on it. We were gonna meet you at Iguana Grill, right?

"Absolutely! I need a good margarita. And I sure need y'all's company. I'll get ready and see you there. The Fru Frus are coming this afternoon to get the decorations finished."

"And me and Gus are gonna be getting' the outside ready for them Fru Frus. I'll be outside if y'all need me. Gus is on his way."

"Elegance is fixin' to hit the Cartwright mansion, honey. I'm so happy for you. It's all gonna be alright. I can fix it." Blake said as she hugged me tight before she put on her black cashmere long coat and headed back out into the crisp December air.

"Thanks sweetie. I do feel so much better," I smiled.

"Me too," Jack added. He looked a little frazzled. "I'll be right behind you, Blake. See ya when we get there." He gave her a thankful hug as she stepped out the back steps toward her car.

Jack and I stood alone in the kitchen. Both of us inhaled a deep breath, as if in a rhythm of anxiety. A heavy stillness enveloped us as we looked at each other, worry in our eyes. I smiled first, then patted the oversized island. "Want another go at it—maybe tomorrow? Hell by then all of this will be water under the bridge. I trust Blake." I tried to sound positive, change the solemn mood filling the room.

Jack stroked my hair, tangling his fingers in the loose strands. He gazed at me before he spoke. "No matter what. Marci can't change a thing. I'm the happiest I have ever been. You in my arms—that is seriously all I need in this world." He kissed me and left through the front door. I walked to the front hall and stood in front of that huge tree. Peering out the window, I watched him drive away.

I climbed the stairs to get ready for my lunch with the girls. My legs were heavy. I had to admit, Marci had me nervous. I knew the media would eat this story up. But if we could manage to nip it in the bud before she could show the divorce papers on TV, we could stop her in her tracks.

I felt sure she couldn't do a thing to stop the big Christmas Gala. It had already taken on a life of its own. The list was complete, the RSVPs had already come in and been noted. All of the big University elite and Tuscaloosa's top class were coming, along with many family friends. Dallas had promised to do a great story as a favor weeks ago. I think they had planned a live remote since it was Tuscaloosa's first B&B in an historic home.

I began to pick apart what Marci could really do to ruin things. Maybe nothing. But one thing was for sure. I had to make sure her reservation for a room here was somehow *lost.* I smiled to myself as I thought of Drew and his redneck cousins.

CHAPTER 15

I pulled into the parking lot at the Iguana Grill in Midtown. I loved the cute outdoor shopping mall. It was sweetly decorated in classy white lights and a huge Christmas tree stood at the center of all the upscale shops. And honey, the best cupcakes anywhere on earth were right here across from the restaurant—Gigi's. My mouth was already watering. The Christmassy cupcakes were all displayed in the window, which was decorated with red gingham curtains and tied back with velvet green bows. Gingerbread men were hanging from a cute clothesline across the front window. It was the most adorable Christmas window I had ever seen! Their Christmas cupcakes were so creative. Everything from Christmas trees and reindeer and of course snowmen—all made of icing. As I pulled into my parking spot, the pink and green writing pulled me in. Gigi's was catering at my Gala, and that made me smile, forgetting all about Marci for a moment. Cupcakes just have that effect of me. Especially Gigi's.

I was dressed in black pants and a Christmassy red turtleneck sweater, my pearls dangling from my ears and my wrist. I wore a long old-fashioned strand doubled around my neck. Very classy. I had poofed my hair with hairspray and pulled it into a low bun at the nape of my neck, and curled it so it could hang loosely around my face. I made sure that in case Marci had followed me, I could feel ready to face her. Maybe I was a tad insecure. Just a tad.

Vivi pulled in right next to me. I smiled at her as we both got out. The chill in the mid-day air actually felt good, a fresh breath was just what I needed. It was only early afternoon and it had already ben an action-packed day. Already Coco had shown up with about 15 elves and was planning a "routine" (whatever that meant), then, Jack and I had our little "tasting" session, followed by threats from his ex-wife. I was exhausted and we still had to finish all the decorating in a couple of hours. I was starting to look forward to Christmas Day, when things would be quiet, the inn would be nearly empty and I could take the tent down on the circus that had become my life.

I got out of my car and waited for Vivi, as I straightened my clothes. She grabbed her black Michael Kors leather bag from the passenger seat and slammed her car door shut as she stepped out.

"Hey Honey, don't you look fab!" She made her way over to my car and gave me a hug as I shut my door.

Blake pulled in on the other side of me, waving as she shifted into park. I had gotten a new hounds-tooth scarf and had it draped over my shoulders. The wind shot a gust of cold across me so I wrapped it up around my neck a little tighter. It worked to calm my nerves as much as warm my face.

"Oooh, love that wrap! I see you are in the Crimson Tide spirit now that you've moved back here." Blake stopped abruptly as she looked at my eyes. "Oh honey, it's gonna be okay. I see that look in your eyes and I've already sent a request for copies of the records. Let's get you a drink the minute we get inside," Blake said, her motherly side appearing as she draped her warm comforting arm around me.

"Y'all gonna have to fill me in on all this," Vivi insisted as she walked next to me. "But whatever it is, honey, we can fix it. Blake and I have fixed so much crap over the last few years, there's pretty much nothin' we can't figure out."

"I'll toast to that—in about five minutes. C'mon ladies, let's get in out of this cold. I love the atmosphere in this place. We have two hours before Rhonda has to be home for the Fru Frus. I'm starved." Blake stepped ahead and opened the door for both Vivi and me.

We all walked inside Iguana's in Midtown. I had only been here once before to meet Jack just before Thanksgiving. This place was certainly gorgeous so it fit the bill. Today we were all in the mood for *fancy.*

We walked inside and I felt immediately transported to another place. The beautiful lighting sparkled in the trees, all the lighted twinkling stars dangled from the ceiling, and the murals were just gorgeous. I relaxed instantly. Blake led the way to a rounded table near the back where the well-dressed waiter met us with the drink menu.

"Honey, we don't need that menu—three margaritas please, on the rocks with salt. And hurry." She giggled, trying to change the serious mood I had been in since she saw me at the mansion.

"Yes, Sugar, hurry," Vivi pushed with a grin. "We're so thirsty!" She laughed. We all settled in as Blake filled Vivi in on Marci and her current manipulations.

"Good God almighty! Is there anything this woman won't do to get what she wants?"

"That's just the thing—what is it that she wants?" I asked. "Surely she has no real interest in the inn."

"No, I know for sure that's not it. She's using this to get Jack's attention," Blake surmised.

"But why in the world would she still be interested in Jack? She was the one who had the affair. What a damn fool. I never did like her." Vivi snarled.

I loved Vivi. She was just what I needed. A dose of Vivi and a margarita. That'll fix anything. The waiter arrived with chips and salsa and three salty thick glasses of the sweet, sour concoction. "To Rhonda and Jack and to the Southern Comforts Inn and to Marci getting' what's coming to her. Cheers!" Vivi made the first toast of the afternoon and we all raised our glasses with a laugh.

How's the party plannin' comin'" Vivi asked chomping down on a chip.

"It's all pretty set, I think. I have the whole RSVP list completed, the food is all bought, recipes ready to go. I have asked Abby and Annie to help me prepare some of the pre-cooked recipes and of course the Fru Frus are bringing food to the house on Friday morning too. I have ten dozen cupcakes from Gigi's coming too!

I put the Fru Frus in charge of most of the hors d'oeuvres and I have the bar being tended by some cutie-pie male bartenders Annie knows. I really feel like I have good control of the Gala. Coco and Jean-Pierre have found a five piece Orchestra, and y'all get this, Coco showed up on the front lawn early this morning with an entire sleigh-full of elves!"

"What? Elves? Like real elves? Like Oompa Loompas?" Vivi laughed as she licked the side of her margarita glass.

"The exact same. Honey, they were turning cartwheels and doing back flips before eight o'clock this morning! I thought I was having a North Pole nightmare." I grabbed a chip and bit into the crunchy salt.

"Lord, you never know what those two are gonna do. Once they have an idea, it will usually manifest somewhere."

"They've also hired Victorian Dickens style carolers to stroll around and sing," I added.

"Oh, now I love that idea," Blake nodded as she chewed. "That goes right along with the whole elegance theme you're doing. Perfect."

The waiter took our orders quickly and left, soon returning with some iced teas and more chips and salsa. We were laughing and relaxing. Sure felt better than I had after the unannounced Marci visit. For a moment I actually forgot about all the crap facing me with her in town. Then a reminder walked in.

"Oh honey, the devil herself has arrived," Vivi whispered.

"Y'all stay quiet. Let me see who that is she's with. I don't want her to see us. It's our turn to spy on her," Blake proposed, her eyebrow up.

We all kinda sunk down in our seats. Quiet took over the space as we all sat watching her.

"Oh my y'all did you see that? She kissed that dude on the cheek before she headed to the ladies room," Vivi noticed.

"Quiet! Shhh! She'll see us," Blake demanded sliding down even further in her seat.

"That man is as old as Santa—and he looks kinda like him too. He's way too old for Marci. She can't be seeing him romantically," I conceded.

"Wait! That's one of my colleagues. He's an attorney," Blake squinted her eyes to get a better look.

Marci sashayed back to their table and scooted into her seat. Their waiter showed up and lingered giving Vivi and me a chance to stare without being noticed. Her lunch date was older, with short white beard. Heavy-set with little glasses.

"Okay, y'all I give. That *is* freakin' Santa. Maybe she's sharing her Christmas list over lunch."

"That's certainly not Santa. That's Lyndon Guthrie. He's the sleaziest lawyer in town. His ethics have always been in question," Blake informed. A lot of my friends in the legal circles want him disbarred. He's always fighting for the wrong side. And he'll just about do anything to win. Like I said; sleazy."

Guthrie. The name stuck in my head. I knew that name. I searched my mind, remembering when I was little and hearing Granny Cartwright talk about *that Guthrie woman.* That was how she referred to the lady. I knew she didn't like that family. I told Blake.

"I remember that too," Blake confirmed. "From when I was a little girl, Meridee used to say, those Guthrie's and Cartwright's put the Hatfield's and the McCoy's to shame. There was some sorta feud, I think." Blake and Vivi were still hunched down in her seat, not to be noticed.

Why would she be with a Guthrie? Maybe it was all just a coincidence. But I did know he was a lawyer. That alone was enough. Because I knew the legal issues she was facing—and they all had to do with me, and everything I held dear. She was most definitely after something, I surmised to myself. But what exactly, I wasn't totally sure.

Just then I heard a loud noise.

"Somebody wanna help me up from down here?"

I tuned in a start to see Vivi under the table. She had slid so far down in her chair it had tipped her chair over and thrown her to the floor. Of course, Marci looked directly over to us, only to get a full view of my very round ass bent over to help Vivi up.

"Good, lord woman! You barely even had half a glass yet! Blake giggled as she jumped up to help.

"And you're already under the table! I hate to see it when you've had a couple," I teased. "Here grab my hand." I reached for Vivi under the table, sprawled out like a banana peel on concrete.

Marci and her "date" got a full on view of my rear. No matter what I did, I reconciled, I was just gonna be at my worst every time that bimbo looked my way. I decided to let her know I saw her too.

But it sure looked like she didn't wanna be seen by us either.

She quickly yanked up the menu to cover her face. Then the man reached over and motioned for her to put it down. He saw that we were looking their way. They didn't want to be noticed, it was clear. But he was trying to play it cool. They glanced at us again— fidgeting uncomfortably.

"Y'all it looks like we got us a voyeur. Let's let'er know we see her too and we don't freakin' care," Vivi muttered hauling herself, in the most un-lady-like manner, spreading her legs to get up from the floor. Ready Blake?" She smiled at me like that was normal for her to fall on the floor. Vivi grabbed her glass, and gave us both a nod. So Blake and I picked up our margarita glasses and toasted Marci from across the room. Then Vivi flipped her off with a grin. I love Vivi. Totally uninhibited.

"Now we're talkin'," I said. Then I clinked Vivi's glass and swigged.

"To The Sassy Belles," Vivi added. "Nobody's got a thing on us!"

CHAPTER 16

Lunch ended with hugs and goodbyes. I loved these two fabulous sisters. What kind of life could we have built together if I hadn't moved out to L.A.? I had missed so much of their lives but was so grateful that they just folded me right back in with them as soon as I was back in Tuscaloosa. I was the luckiest woman alive to have them for my best friends. I know what it feels like now to not be alone in this world. I knew I would always have them to share the good and the bad. That was such a comfort to have my people around me again. Especially Jack.

As I drove my head swam in thoughts. I was more confused than ever now that I saw Marci with that sleazy lawyer. Maybe she had gotten her own attorney so she could fight Jack for what she demanded was her share of the inn.

All I could think of was Jack. I wanted to tell him what happened. Marci looked so uncomfortable and tense from the second she saw us. She was most definitely up to something. I called Jack and told him all about lunch and Marci and Mr. Guthrie.

"Guthrie?" He asked, stopping me mid conversation.

"Yes, Guthrie. Do you know them? Granny Cartwright always despised that family," I added.

"Rhonda, pull over for a second. I'm going on the air soon but I have to tell you something."

"Okay. Why?"

"I know those people. I just had no idea your family knew them.

What all do you remember about them?"

"I know they were always in some sort of feud with my grandmother's family. I'll have to ask mother what the deal was. Why? What do you know?"

"Are you stopped? I just don't want you driving while we talk."

I pulled into Glendale Gardens, just down Hargrove road and not too far from Midtown. Meridee, Blake's grandmother, lived in this old historic neighborhood. Come to think of it, she was a good friend of my granny so she might know something about the Guthries too. I sat parked in front of the little white house with the big screened front porch and the green awnings "Okay babe, I'm stopped. Tell me what you know. Is that big ol' Mr. Guthrie the real Santa Claus? Or the Grinch?"

"No. He's certainly not Santa, that's for sure. Mr. Lyndon Guthrie is Marci's uncle."

"Really? Okay so what would that mean?" I inquired.

"His wife, Voncile Guthrie was Marci's grandmother. That sleazy Lyndon is her oldest son. They were always trying to sue people out of their rights, their property and all their assets. Marci tried to distance herself from them."

I was silent. All I could hear was my own breathing.

"Babe? You there?"

"I'm here, just trying to process this. So really, what is she after? You, or my house, or both?" I was suddenly seeing just what that heifer was up to—and sounding like my own grandmother. That was the country way in the south—if you couldn't stand a female, they almost always became referred to as a heifer.

"Maybe both." Jack informed. "Those people want what other people have and they try to twist the law so they can steal anything they want. Marci always hated them. She said they ruined her reputation in Tuscaloosa."

"Yeah, uh huh, and here she was at lunch in plain sight with the dirtiest lawyer in town." I pursed my lips together and decided to pay Meridee a visit. I hung up with Jack and called Blake and told her everything Jack had said. Then I called Vivi to see if she could meet the Fru Frus and let them inside the inn to start decorating. The day was slipping away but if we were gonna nip this—it had to be now. Every minute that ticked by brought us closer to the Christmas Gala and nothing was gonna mess that party up.

I pulled into Meridee's old cracked driveway. The last time I was here just a few months ago was the day I had found out my Daddy wasn't my Daddy. I learned my mother had had an affair with my uncle, my Daddy's brother—producing me. Yes, my real father was the man I called Uncle Ron all of my life. Daddy died a few months ago but Uncle Ron had disappeared years ago. Just this past September I sat inside this house with my sisters and Blake and Vivi as Meridee helped me see everything in a new light and calmed my anger at my mother. I loved Meridee. She was always the original Sassy Belle. Everyone who knew her loved her. Her house was always open and warm, just like Meridee herself. And I knew she could help me think and she may even have some new details.

I slid out of the front seat of my car and went up the red brick steps off the driveway to her back door. No one ever knocked at Meridee's. If you were a back door guest you were family. Only people who didn't know her went to the front porch.

"Miss Meridee? You home? It's Rhonda Cartwright."

"Hey baby! What in the world brings you by today? Merry Christmas!" She leaned in and gave me a hug, all five feet of her. She was such a tiny woman, about eighty-three years old and maybe 115 pounds. Her blue eyes sparkled when she saw me. Meridee loved company, even unannounced.

"Wanna a Coke? I got Krispy Kremes over here on the corner cabinet, help yourself." This was Meridee. She had been this way the whole time I had known her. Blake and Vivi and I had been friends all through Catholic grade school at St. Catherine's—so I had known Meridee my whole life. But today, it was her friendship with my grandmother that I was most interested in. I smiled and grabbed a doughnut as I took my seat across from the stove near her fridge.

I sat down at her yellow laminate 1950s kitchen table in the center of the cozy space and filled her in on all the details. She grabbed us both a Coke and sat down across from me. Blake popped in just as Meridee took her seat and made herself comfortable at the end of the table.

"Hey Nanny," Blake said leaning over to give her grandmother a hug and a kiss. Meridee started to get up. "No. No, Nanny—I got it. Don't get up," she grinned knowing Meridee had to get everyone a cold Coke, so Blake got herself a Coke, in glass bottles of course, from the 1940s fridge on the back porch and sat down at the end of the table.

"Well my lands sakes! This sure does sound like those Guthries," Meridee popped "Your Granny sure had years of trouble with them," Meridee said to me sipping on her coke.

"Tell me about that. All I could remember was that she really didn't like Mrs. Guthrie," I prodded.

"Oh yeah, honey. None of us liked that Voncile. She was a slut from way back," Meridee blurted.

That made me laugh. Meridee always said just what she thought. She continued.

"See, Voncile and your granny both wanted a lot of the same things. They both wanted that opulent lifestyle, a grand house and a good-looking successful man. But your granny was a cutie-pie. She had a fun personality and all the boys loved her. I can't say the same for that heifer, Voncile."

It seems like that was Voncile's new full name, *that heifer, Voncile.*

"She was just unfortunate, you know, in the looks department." Meridee smiled through her understatement. "The feud started from the day they met. By the time they both married, it had become an all-out battle. Voncile married a pauper who had a drinking problem. Then it all blew up. Her Daddy died and in his will he had been left some land that butted up against the Cartwright property. The mansion you now own. But in true form, those Guthries wanted more than what they actually owned. They kept taking your grandparents to court trying to prove they owned part of the land and the house."

"I remember that case," Blake said. "We actually studied that one in law school. But that was settled long ago. All of that land and the mansion belonged to the Cartwrights, free and clear."

"Exactly," Meridee confirmed. "But that is the very reason the feud has kept going all these years. Those Guthries believe they were robbed and over time they have been trying to find a way to get what they think is theirs."

"Well, honey, I think we get the whole picture now. That heifer Marci is here doing her uncles dirty work," Blake hissed.

"I guess that name just runs in the family. Heifer," I smirked.

"If the shoe fits…" Meridee sassed taking a slow swig of her Coke.

"Touché," we both nodded back at her.

I got up and walked around the table and kissed Meridee. I couldn't express how much better I felt knowing the most important thing—Marci had no interest in Jack. Okay so she wanted my house and my business but not my man. I actually breathed a sigh of relief and felt a smile slip across my face.

" So, Blake—does that mean I'm in the clear?" I asked hopefully.

"Well, it does so far as the house is concerned—but then it gets a little messy."

The smile left my lips and my stomach twisted. "What do you mean, messy?"

"If those divorce papers she's carrying around are real and Jack decides to sign, then she will try to go after his fifty-percent. Remember, she is trying to avenge her family by taking what your family left you. She is motivated to push this. She will be relentless and make his life and yours a living hell. It's not like we can negotiate her away from the inn. That is all she's after. But we can prove that Jack got the house without any loans. She's making this hundred year old battle now about you and her.

Jack bought half of your share of it under his own will—not given a loan based on his football fame. All of that will take time and money to prove. But the real key will be for us to prove that Jack has already signed divorce papers so that new little property clause is not real. That whole divorce packet she is carrying around is false. My God, Rhonda, doesn't he have a copy of his own divorce?"

"I know he's looking. He moved here about a year ago and still has some of his office stuff in boxes around his house."

"Blake! I think we may have a case we can use against her.

Maybe we can get her to drop this whole thing," Meridee interrupted with a huge grin on her face. She set her glass down on the table with a clank. A look on her face that just screamed, "Gotcha!"

"What Meridee, what?" I asked excited and hopeful.

"If Marci is anything like her grandmother, she's a dumbass. She'll do anything her uncle is asking her to do without even thinking. And she is an opportunist too so if she thinks this would be good for her in the long run, she'll be ready to do it. And I *know* he knows better. But I was married to one of the very best attorneys this state has ever seen: my Frank. And one time he had him a case where somebody was trying to blackmail his client. He had created all this paperwork and buried in it all was a clause handing everything over. The pressure was unbearable and Frank's client almost signed over the family fortune without even knowing it."

"I think I see exactly where you're going with this, Nanny. You shoulda been a lawyer yourself," Blake assured.

"Will somebody tell me please?" I was totally confused.

"Nanny, you do the honors, " Blake said as if she were handing over the floor to a colleague.

"It's a crime in the state of Alabama to falsify a legal document. And last I looked divorce papers are legal documents. Marci could get a hefty fine and maybe even some jail time if we can prove those papers aren't real."

"Oh I love it," I yelped.

"And we don't really even have to prove anything," Blake added. "I could threaten her with some fines and jail time and see if I can get her to cave. I'll call her first thing in the morning and ask her to come by the office. This is gonna be good."

"Y'all are pure geniuses. How can I ever thank you?"

"Well, it's not totally over but this sure gives us a leg up. Now stop worrying and go home and help those Fru Frus before they find a live manger scene for the front yard," Blake teased. "Nanny, you have saved the day as usual. What would any of us ever do without you?" Blake stood up and leaned down to kiss her grandmother goodbye. "I love you."

"I love you too." I smiled. "I can't wait to tell Jack!"

"Y'all be good and lemme know what happens," Meridee answered back. "My Frank was damn good. Blake, you take after him. He would be so proud of you."

"I know, Nanny. He was the reason I wanted to go to law school in the first place. Call ya later." Blake blew Meridee another kiss as both of us made our way out the back door and to our cars. I thanked Blake and gave her a hug and headed to the mansion. Relief washed over me and I felt hopeful for the first time in so long.

I looked at the time on my car dashboard and I knew Jack was on the air with his bulldog, Bear. I listened to his deep sexy voice. I remembered what Meridee said. Basically that Marci was a dumbass. I certainly agreed with *that*. She let Jack Bennett go. That alone proved just how much of a dumbass she really was. And now, jail might be in her future. I recalled all the modeling Marci did when she was younger. All that good fashion sense. Ha! Whoever knew orange would wind up being her new favorite color?

CHAPTER 17

It had gotten late. Four in the afternoon, darkness already closing in. I pulled into the drive and saw the unmistakable Pepto Bismal pink van that was known all over town as the Fru Frus'. Vivi's powder blue little Thunderbird was parked along the street out front. Anybody in town would know exactly who was at the mansion. I got out and dropped my keys into my cream Coach bag and made my way to the front porch.

The activity in the house was frenetic. You could hear the rolling laughter and the high-pitched excited talking from outside. Christmas music floated from the windows. It was a live Norman Rockwell picture. I stood still for a moment to take it in. Coco was up on top of a ladder working on the curved bannister, his bright red pants visible. He held a long flare of red velvet ribbon, and he was singing loudly. I could make out some words and the melody. I could see Vivi laughing, her bright Christmas green turtleneck the perfect backdrop for her coppery auburn hair. Jean-Pierre was holding his iPad and pointing to the stairs.

I loved all the music and activity in the mansion. Watching it through the windows made me so nostalgic. Granny would be so happy to see this. I glanced over to the side of the porch where my planter of dandelions had been growing in September. The winter cold had taken them all for now but I knew Gus would bring them back for me in the spring. If I could wish on one right now I would wish Marci would just go away. Other than that, all my wishes had already come true. Then I remembered—she'd be staying right here at the inn in just two nights. I had to put a stop to that.

"Hey y'all. I'm finally home," I announced as I walked inside. I stood totally motionless. Frozen. It was stunning. The two-story was glittering in Christmas lights, hundreds of golden twinkling bulbs, tracing up the handrail of the curved staircase. The bannister was draped in real greenery and white lights, red velvet fabric laced throughout the fragrant branches. Scents of cinnamon and pine filled my nostrils. It was like another place in time. Oversized candelabras set as centerpieces and filled with crimson tapered candles on the chests on either side of the dining hall. Real greenery was everywhere, draped over all the fireplaces. Every nook of the mansion was dotted with baby's breath making it look like fresh fallen snowflakes had just floated down from the sky. I was in a Christmas wonderland.

"Hey sugar! Girl, dontcha just love it? I mean if I do say so myself." Coco climbed down the ladder with a wide grin.

"Oh, Coco! I love it! It is exactly what I was hoping for—such sophistication and elegance. I feel like I'm in a dream."

Vivi appeared from the kitchen with Jean-Pierre. Both of them had a meatball on a toothpick. "Oh hey, Rhonda. Isn't this all just lovely?" Vivi asked. "Have a meatball."

"I love it so much. Thank y'all." But then I noticed that the tree was still bare. I wanted to mention it but didn't want to sound pushy. They were still working.

"Come in here," Vivi suggested leading the way back into the kitchen. "I wanna go over some of these delicious appetizers. These things are sure better 'an any balls I ever had!" She laughed at her own joke. Plus you gotta see all the guest rooms. You are gonna just die they are all so Christmassy. These boys have totally outdone themselves."

"I can't wait," I said following right behind Vivi.

I had made the menu with Jean Pierre a week ago. I was making a few of my specialties but he was doing the majority of the work. Behind the kitchen I had Drew build me a back room for my extra refrigerators and freezers for the inn. The large kitchen was decked out in Christmas decorations of a bygone era. The space was ablaze in red gingham and real greenery. Wreathes made of cedar and pinecones hung in the center of every window and above the over-sized cream-colored fireplace which anchored the kitchen on the left wall. Greenery draped over the mantel and the red checked fabric was tied in huge bows around the backs of all the high stools at the island, in the center at the top of all the wreathes, and all along the tops of the antique white cabinetry throughout. My kitchen was very French country.

The massive chandelier over the island displayed round peppermint candies hanging from each wrung around the edges, each tied in a red bow. The hard smooth island itself had a gingerbread house complete with Mr. and Mrs. Santa flanked on either side, all of the pieces sitting atop large pedestal cake plates. The whole place was warm and wonderful. Fire blazed in the fireplace and created an air of the past, when times were so much simpler. When Granny would be in here singing, asking me to help her decorate the cookies. I was overcome.

"Oh y'all this is just spectacular. I am so thrilled I just don't even know what to say. It's just wonderful."

"All the ingredients for the menu items are here and waiting." Jean-Pierre informed. "I'll come over on Thursday and fix everything while you make your specialties."

"What a shin-dig huh? This is pure ol' dee fab-u-lous!" Coco added a melody as he sang out his opinions. He was so wonderful. I just had to pray the events he had planned for outside were gonna be just as tasteful. The thought of those elves had me more than a tad worried. I suddenly shuttered as images of a Christmas circus filled my head.

After the entire tour of the inn, all the rooms as tasteful as the one before, I was back downstairs standing at the bare tree. I looked up at it and inhaled deeply hoping they would say something. Coco jumped right in.

"Oh, sweetie, we decided not to do your tree. I mean of course we will finish it off for you with the final trimmings so it will match the rest of the house."

"Why aren't y'all doing it along with everything else?" I questioned.

"Don't you wanna decorate your tree with Jack, or your sisters? Trees are so personal. And decorating them with your closest family is the way it should be. That's how memories of Christmas are created. Everyone has such special memories of homemade decorations, strung popcorn, you know, it's just personal."

Tears filled my eyes. I looked around. All the fireplaces were lit. The sun had finally set and darkness crept inside the floor to ceiling window frames. The house was brimming with warmth and the sweet spirit of Christmas. I had memories of decorating our Christmas trees with Granny, my Daddy and Uncle Ron. My mom would bring food and Granny would fill the tables with sweet sugared concoctions from her kitchen. Rum and bourbon balls, chess squares, peanut butter pie, pecan pie; loads of mouth-watering deliciousness! We'd sing as Daddy and Uncle Ron played the music. Abby and Annie and I would dance around the grand piano. We strung real popcorn for the tree and weeks before Christmas, Granny would give us a needle and thread and she would send us to the dining room table to sew. We always sang Christmas carols while we sewed the strands of popcorn together, the fireplace in the dining room crackling.

That memory gave me the most brilliant idea. I would plan a decorating party with Abby and Annie, and then Jack and I would decorate the tree tomorrow night. Annie's show was late in the day and Abby surely could drop by for an hour or so. I'd call them both and set it up. I was nearly shaking thinking I could actually re-create some childhood memories right here in our family home! The excitement thrilled me.

"Y'all are so right! Thank you so much for thinking of this. I'll make a plan and then on Thursday when you get here to do the hors d'oeuvres, y'all can finish it up."

"Perfect. Well, we'll let you get some sleep. It's been a long day," Jean-Pierre hugged me tightly. Coco and Vivi did the same. All those hugs felt so wonderful. It was just so good to be home at last—home in this house, the very heart of my childhood. I was finally building a real life. Tonight, I really would have visions of sugarplums dancing in my head.

But I knew it was times like these that, I would usually just wait on the other shoe to drop. I knew one thing; it better not be a familiar crimson high heel!

CHAPTER 18

I woke up on Wednesday morning with renewed hope and excitement. I showered and dressed for the day, called both of my sisters about stringing popcorn, called Jack and filled him in on Blake's plans and made a date with him to decorate the big tree. It was gonna be a fabulous day. I literally skipped down the gorgeous decorated stairs and headed into the most Christmassy kitchen on the planet.

I like the real kind of popcorn so I grabbed the jar and the oil and turned on the gas chef's stove. I went into the sewing drawers and got the needles and thread and when the popcorn was finished, I arranged everything on the dining room table. Of course I had buttery popcorn for us to snack on while we sewed. Real butter is the only way to cook down south—two ingredients in real butter: cream, and salt. Delicious! And so perfect!

I had made a fire in the dining room fireplace. It was such a cozy room even though the table could seat fourteen people, enough for breakfast for my guests in the inn. The gray dreary day set the mood with the heavy bloated clouds hanging over the spiky leafless trees. More freezing rain and sleet was on the way as icy wind kicked the bare tree limbs against the sides of the house. I had to admit, I already loved this day and it had barely started. It was the kind of day that begged for a homemade soup to sit simmering on the stove all day long, filling the house with the scent of herbs, and roasted chicken. I wanted to cook, to nest, to be in my own home, ready to open the doors and welcome people inside. I knew this was just what I meant to do. Food is love, some say, and maybe that was why I became a chef in the first place; I was missing the love that used to fill the house. Now by serendipity, it was my place to fill it again, just like my granny did the whole time I was growing up here. And it felt good—to be in this spot, to be the one to not only save and restore the family home, but to save and restore the family.

Just then I saw another little box, this time wrapped in red and sitting on the windowsill near the banquette. I sat down and opened it. A dainty charm bracelet. Now I could wear the charm I had gotten. *Who in the world is doing this?* I wondered to myself. Maybe it was Drew. It might even be Vivi. Whoever it was, I kinda liked it—like having a real secret Santa. I decided to keep this one to myself. Maybe he or she would reveal themselves—or better yet, I could catch them in the act.

My cell rang and I pulled it out of my sweater pocket. The caller ID announced Blake. My easiness turned into queasiness.

"Hello?"

"Hey Rhonda, okay, here's the deal." She cut right to it. "The public records in Boston aren't showing a divorce for Jack on file. They are doing an extended search just to make sure and will get back to me in a day or so. Meanwhile, get Jack to look through all those boxes."

"Oh no, what does this mean?" I asked nervously wiping my hands on a yellow-checked dishcloth near the simmering soup.

"Well it just means we need to look a little harder. Make sure he has given me the right county. The records may be stored in a different location. Getting Marci on falsifying documents is our best bet, and I can try to scare her when she comes here today. "Oh, did you get her?"

"Yep. She'll be here in an hour. I'll fill you in when I finished with her. Maybe I can kill two birds with one stone."

'Whadya mean?"

"I think if I can get her to admit her sleazy uncle has put her up to this, I can finally throw that freak in jail—something I have wanted to do to Lyndon Guthrie for as long as I can remember. I plan to offer her a deal to turn him in on the illegal records. We'll see. I'll keep ya posted."

"Ok, I'll be here today. Got lots to do to get ready for this weekend. Call me as soon as she leaves. And Blake—thanks. I really mean that."

"Of course, we're all family now and we all want that house to stay in the family. Talk to ya later. Don't worry. It'll be fine."

She hung up. I pressed my cell to my chest and smiled to myself. Blake was right. Somehow it would all work out. It had to.

I decided to make more of that chicken soup to freeze. I had about forty-five minutes to chop the vegetables and get the broth going, boil and chop the chicken. Savory was the perfect flavor for today's frigid temps and wind. I even decided to make some homemade cornbread. The doorbell rang just as I stuck the cornbread into the oven. My sisters were both standing outside, in the cold.

"Y'all get in here, let's get this party started," I announced as I flung open the old doors.

"Oh Rhonda," Abby said as she stood in the grand foyer. She was staring up at the staircase, and glancing into the side parlors. "This totally reminds me of when we were little." Abby looked at me, tears glistened in her eyes. Annie couldn't even speak; her emotions flowed down her cheeks.

"I know, y'all. I love it too. I felt the same way when I got here yesterday. The whole time they were decorating it was such a mess, but now, with it all done, well—it just feels so transporting."

"Yeah, back to when life was so sweet." Annie wiped her cheek.

The girls took off their coats and scarves and threw their boots to the side of the front door. They padded, stocking footed, to the huge dining table and sat down in front of the large bowls of popcorn. The fireplace crackled and the songs began. Happiness encased us for an hour until—the doorbell rang.

"Expecting someone else at our little party?" Annie asked with her eyebrows up.

"No. I sure didn't invite anyone else," I answered, getting up from my spot in front of the fireplace. I walked over to the door and peered out the window. Mother. *No*, I thought to myself. *Why now?*

Of all times?

"It's Mother, y'all." I shook my head.

"Great," Abby said, her mood changing in an instant.

"There goes all the fun," Annie added.

All of us were still pretty angry at mother for keeping secrets about her affair with our uncle. When we all found out I was only a half sister to the both of them it just stung to the core. Mother had been having a decade long affair with Daddy's brother right under her husband's nose. All the secrets were buried here in the house and when I inherited it, I found all the evidence. Maybe that was really why Daddy had left the place to me. So to say we really weren't ready to have Mother at our decorating party was an understatement.

"Yep—here we go. Sorry y'all," I said as I moved to open the door.

"Wait! Maybe we can get rid of her," Abby suggested. "Annie, grab your bowl and run in the kitchen." They both jumped up and ran to the kitchen, popcorn flying from the bowls, both of them slipping in the stocking feet. They rounded the corner and hid out in the kitchen pantry while I answered the door shoving popcorn from the table into my mouth.

"Oh, hey, Mother. What are you doing here?" I asked innocently.

"I just wanted to drop by and check in on you. I been shoppin' and have a few little things I thought you might like." She set down a bag and started pulling out Christmas ornaments and displayed them on the dining table. Then she stopped to look around. Mother never missed a thing. She was so used to living as a sneaky woman, she was always on the lookout to make sure she never got caught with my Uncle Ron.

"Well, the Fru Frus have sure restored the beauty of this place at Christmastime. It really brings back a lot of memories." She stood still for a minute, taking everything in—and then, "Is somebody else here?"

"No, why do you ask?" I said with a gulp. I mean it wasn't that we didn't want her there, it was just that well—we didn't really want her there.

"I see popcorn on the floor and needles and thread."

"Oh, I was just making a string of popcorn for the tree."

"Why do you need three needles?" She kept pushing. Then she glanced to the front door and saw the pile of boots behind the door on the floor. "Who's here?"

Abby and Annie scuffled around, making noise, just as Mama entered the kitchen.

"I knew it. Why in the world are y'all hidin' from me? Y'all didn't want me here did you? Why? Why would y'all not want me here?" She seemed like the last girl to be picked for grade-school kickball.

I should have felt sad that I had hurt her but for some reason I was mad. Mad that she was wreaking my little party and mad that she was making me feel bad.

"Look, Mother, I just wanted Abby and Annie here for today. You're coming to the Gala. Today was for me and my sisters to re-create some new memories, that's all." I was so trying to be nice. But I felt a fit comin' on.

"Well why the hell wouldn't you wanna make new memories with me too? I'm part of this family too, in case you forgot."

"No, Mama, I certainly have not forgotten. But you are the one who made all those choices way back and we just needed some girl time. We need to remember what made us sisters to start with—not just that we thought we shared the same mother and daddy but that no matter what we're still us. And since you sorta cause all that doubt, well, we didn't include you for today. I'm just sorry. But what I'm really sorry about is that you hid your dirty little secrets from us and made us feel this way in the first place.

"Fine, I'm gone! I know when I'm not welcome somewhere. I'll go and y'all just have yourselves a merry old time. Why don't you just pretend I'm dead and gone too, like Daddy? He would be so ashamed."

"No Mama, that's where you're wrong—he would be so ashamed of you. Not me."

She was shaking. I had gone too far and I immediately knew that but the words were already out there, shattering the progress both Mother and I had been trying so hard to make in the last few months.

Shattering the warmth of the day I had planned.

She made her way back to the foyer, and turned for one last thing.

"And just to think I was coming to ask you if you had a Santa yet for your party. Just forget the whole thing."

She walked out and slammed the front door, Christmas bells jingling from the knob. I peered out the big window, watching her walk back to her car. She shoved her cold hands deep into her coat pockets as she walked, her head down. I saw her slide into her car and check her reflection in the rearview mirror. She brushed tears from her cheeks with her gloved fingers before she backed out. I turned to face my sisters; the decorations mother left still lying on the table. Tears spilled over my cheeks.

"Oh honey," Annie said slipping her arm around me. "She can ruin things without even trying."

"Rhonda, I know you wanted this to be a special day for us and it was, look at all this popcorn that will go on the tree. I had a wonderful morning with you and Annie. I love you so much for even thinking of this. Don't mind Mother. She'll be okay. She knows she's a pain in the ass. Believe me," Abby consoled.

"And don't forget," Annie reminded us. "Control freaks never like surprises."

" And she is certainly a control freak from way back," I agreed. "But she's hurt. I didn't mean to hurt her, but maybe I did mean it. Oh y'all I wanted so much to get some new memories going." I sniffed as tears filled my eyes. I knew I was wrong.

"You did make us some new memories—and new traditions too. We can do this every year. But, please, plan to serve alcohol next time. It helps with this kind of little surprise.

We finished up with the popcorn and hung the strings up on a curtain to wait for Jack that night. The aroma of the chicken soup floating under our noses, we cleaned up the dining room and the girls got ready to leave. I kissed them both goodbye and headed back in to stir the soup. I stood there in my huge French country kitchen thinking about everything. Then I remembered Mother asked me about Santa Claus. Was she planning on Santa being her plus one? I heaved in a deep breath and kept stirring. I knew one thing—I could sure use me a real Santa about right now.

CHAPTER 19

I felt a little sick to my stomach after Mother left. I had to find a way to really make peace with her—forgive her. Really deep down in my heart and soul, forgiveness was gonna be so hard. Over the last few months, I had been trying but I realized I was just going through the motions getting along with her. Making peace is not the same as true forgiveness. I realized today I had not forgiven her—and worse, I wasn't sure that I could.

I kept myself busy, remembering that Blake was seeing Marci. I felt a clench in my belly as I checked my kitchen clock. It had been more than enough time for Blake to threaten, ahem, *talk,* to Marci. I was wringing my hands, anxiety setting in as the time ticked by. I had plans with Jack so I wanted to get this out of my head. Just as I decided to pick up my phone, I heard a knock at my back door. I ran over and peeked through the curtains to see Blake. This didn't look good.

"Hey honey, get in here. That sleet is picking up." I said welcoming her into the warm kitchen.

"I know you've been waiting for my call. I was out and just thought I'd swing by." Blake stepped in, slinging the melted droplets from her dark coat. She took a deep breath and offered me a consoling smile. Even before she opened her mouth, I knew it probably wasn't good news.

"Well, I grilled that Marci till she almost broke." Blake sat down in the banquette and I brought her a cup of coffee and joined her.

"Tell me everything. What happened?"

Blake took a sip of her coffee and began. "Marci arrived dressed to the nines as usual. She sat down and I began to ask her questions about her marriage to Jack. She said the papers were filed in Norfolk County. Jack and Marci lived in Wellesley, not in Boston proper. So I have contacted their records office now. The real problem is the lawyer that handled their divorce has been disbarred. His offices are closed now. Hopefully they can find something. I couldn't get a thing online but I led Marci to believe I could get everything within a day so she would know I was pushing. I let her know this was a crime if we proved these documents weren't real. But guess what—she brought a copy of the papers with her and I had Wanda Jo make a copy. We now have tangible proof if these papers happen to be fabricated. Meridee was right, she really is a dumbass." We both laughed. Then I thought of something else.

"Unless she really believes those papers are real. Maybe her sleazy uncle is the one who made the papers and convinced her that Jack never signed."

"I sure wouldn't put it past him," she conjectured.

"How did she act?" I inquired

"She seemed really nervous, especially when we talked about the fines, an arrest, and possibly jail. I mean this is not just a falsification of records; this falls into the category of fraud. And that is much worse. Dishonesty calculated for advantage is what that's called. I mean legally speaking it's one thing to falsify a divorce record but that clause that was added about her owning half of all of his future endeavors, that is a whole new ball game. One she's gonna lose big-time."

"God Blake, you're good. I am so lucky to have you. I do feel so much better. I'm still nervous. When will we know something?"

"I hope no later than late tomorrow. I think Marci's gonna cave anyway. And I think you could be right—it's all that low-life she calls an uncle. I think she's gonna go back and talk to him. He may even be low enough to try to blame her. But I could see her start to squirm in my office. There's only one thing that worries me."

"What?"

"Like I said at Meridee's—she seems to see this as her battle now; like her grandmother's fight has been passed down to her. If she can finally be the one to get part of this property into her family, she would be the family heroine. Even though she always wanted separation, now since she is single again, she needs to feel she belongs. It fits the profile."

"A lawyer has to be a psychologist too," I reasoned.

"Well, it sure helps to figure motive. And Marci Miller has plenty of that."

"I'll get Jack and we'll go look for records he still has in boxes tonight. We have a big date planned."

"Oh, do tell. I need to hear something sweet now."

"Well, I making us a simple dinner; chicken soup, some cornbread and a cinnamon pumpkin cobbler with a streusel topping. Then we're gonna decorate the tree together. He's supposed to be here pretty soon."

"Oooh, sounds like a cozy little evening you have planned," she winked.

"I have been excited all day long. Then mother dropped by and wrecked the mood."

"Oh, no. Well don't let her upset you, sweetie."

"This time, it was me that upset her first. She was really hurt. I just feel awful and sick now."

"Honey, listen to me. I can't think of a single Christmas that some family member didn't make a mess of things. Christmas can sometimes make us crazier than we usually are. Expectations will usually cause some sort of disappointment. Let it go. Call her and say you're sorry. But no matter what, do not let this mess up time with Jack. That's the core of happiness sweetheart—that real love you and he have. Now, go get gorgeous!"

"I was on my way up to get gorgeous when you knocked," I flashed her a smile that told her I was gonna be okay.

"Well, don't let me keep you. I just wanted to stop by and get you up to speed. You're gonna be fine. Just give it a day or so and we'll get it nipped, sweetie." She stood up and hugged me bye and left out the kitchen door.

I wiped down the counters and straightened up. I was just fixin' to head upstairs to spruce up when Blake was back knocking again.

"Hey girl, what'd you forget?" I whipped the door open.

"Looks like you're the one who forgot something." Marci was standing right in front of me. "You really are so predictable aren't you? You never check to see who's at the back door but you look out that front door like a guard dog, " she sneered. She was so smug and mean. I wanted to claw her eyes out.

Marci stepped inside, uninvited.

"I went to see your little lawyer BFF today. She thinks she's got this all figured out. But I wanted to stop by and give you a little warning. Unless you call her off, I'll call WTAL and get a story going that you'll never be able to live down. You are shacking up with a married man—and you know how well that'll go over in this town. Your business will be hurt, your name will be mud and Jack will probably lose all his sponsors. If you want to prevent all this, just have him meet me and sign the papers."

"And have you become part owner here? Are you outta your freakin' dumbass mind? No way. I own this place not you. It never belonged to your grandma Voncile or any of the other freaks in your disgusting little clan. You wanna fight me? You like the old family feud? Fine. We can revive it. But just like the rest of my family did, I'll kick your ass from here all the way back to Boston. Now have a nice day."

I walked over to the back door and opened it with a dramatic swing; cold wind and rain blew inside as the wicked witch walked out. "And don't even think about coming back here! You're reservation has been cancelled!"

The minute I slammed the door I broke down in tears, my shoulders shaking. I slid down the back door and squatted on the floor, crying. How much more could I take? I just wanted to run my inn and love Jack. Everyday. That was all. I couldn't believe Marci showed up here and threatened me. Blake was right. Even if her uncle put her up to everything, Marci herself was in it—to become the big family hero.

What if she really would call the TV station? She could really hurt me, not to mention my whole family and Jack. I was trying to be tough but between my fight with Mother and now trying to defend my family with Marci, I was emotionally drained.

"Baby? Where's my girl?"

And then—my hero arrived.

CHAPTER 20

Jack found me on the floor of the kitchen. He sat down with me and held me, stroking my hair. Darkness fell on what was supposed to be my perfect day. He had brought a bright red Amaryllis plant for the banquette table. I filled him in on this horrible day and told him he had to find those divorce papers. I needed this to be over.

"Baby, I need to show you something. I was trying to call you all day long. Where were you?"

"I was here, just having an argument with Mother, then Blake dropped by. It has been such a crap day. I must have left my phone in the dining room. What did you have to show me? Is that why you were calling?"

"So many questions, my little girl," Jack grinned and kissed my nose, looking deeply into my eyes. "I think this just might dry those tears." He stopped and opened his jacket and pulled out a stapled set of papers, a sticky note protruding from the bottom in the back.

"Oh, Jack, is this...?"

"Go ahead and look at the back where the note is," he prodded. "I think it's the Christmas present you've been waiting for."

I flipped to the back and saw the only thing I needed to see—Jack's signature on his divorce papers. I started crying again and leaned into him, hugging him as tight as I could, like I would never let go.

"See, baby, I told you I knew I had those things somewhere," he smiled at me then kissed me with passion, holding both sides of my face in his gentle hands. He kissed me all over my face, his lips brushing my eyelids, my nose, my forehead, finally resting on my mouth. It was a celebration. He held me and we rocked back and forth, still sitting on the kitchen floor. We laughed and kissed some more. Both of us made our way to our knees still holding each other, kissing each other over and over again. I started to laugh as I kept kissing him. "You're mine Jack Bennett. Mine! Mine, Mine, Mine! Forever."

"You're mine Rhonda Cartwright—all mine. And you always have been. I love you so much. This was all we needed. We're free."

"But we have so much to do now," I said.

"Oh, I have lots to do," he teased, kissing my neck, reaching his hands inside my V-neck sweater, cupping my breast, kissing me again.

"No silly, I mean to Marci. I have to call Blake right away. We need to get her copies of those papers immediately. Marci threatened to go to the TV station. Oh, I wanna set her up to fall in public—just like she said she was gonna do to me and you. I need to call Dallas at the station."

"I do like the way you think. She thought she could kill two birds with one stone but then she ran into us. She wanted to take me down and continue this family feud with your family," Jack said. "I guess she thought it was a perfect plan. I know what I think we need to do next though. How 'bout we celebrate my divorce?" Jack grinned as he kissed me, lying me back and removing his shirt.

"Is this gonna be the room where we always make love?" I asked playfully, unzipping his pants. We were lying on the kitchen floor, cuddling in full celebration of our freedom. It was Christmastime, the kitchen fireplace was ablaze and the smell of my cinnamon pumpkin cobbler filled the room. It was raining hard outside, tapping a rhythmic hum on the glass windows.

"Seems like the kitchen is our spot," Jack answered in a slow deep drawl.

"Well, most people do like the bedroom—but hey as long as it's you, any room works for me. Anytime, anywhere." He slipped my sweater off, his hands dragging down my ribcage as he kissed the mounds of flesh spilling from my bra.

He was hungry. We decided to have dessert first. Maybe this time we'd actually get to the finish line.

"I have never loved anyone like I love you," he whispered, kissing my neck. He was soft and genuine in his way. His words resonated over me. I felt him press his hands under the waistband of my leggings and pull them down, over my round smooth hips and to my knees. He stuck his foot between my knees and pushed them the rest of the way off, shoving them to the side in a heap. "I just learned that trick from somebody. I think I've pretty much mastered that one."

He unhooked my bra and slipped it from beneath me. I felt the flat plane of his hard chest on my now bare breasts, our flesh pressed into one, moving as one... His heart beat next to mine now, in the same frenetic, rapid rhythm. Our breaths ragged on each other's skin. He grasped the back of my head, pulling me toward him and pressed my mouth to his, and held me—driving out worry and anxiety and fear in that long, devouring kiss. His lips brushed against my nipple, his tongue finding a familiar path around the flesh between my breasts. He parted my legs as I made it easy, wrapping my naked thighs around his.

Jack was an intense lover and every time I made love with him the bond just seemed to grow between us. But this time was different. It didn't seem to matter that I looked awful, make-up smeared from crying, that my sweater had a stain from making cornbread or that I smelled a little like onions from making my soup. It didn't matter that we were on the kitchen floor. All I knew was that Jack's weight felt perfect on top of me, that his lips felt like they were right where they belonged, brushing against mine, that my face felt at home in the crook under his jaw, breathing in his skin. Everything felt right in this moment. The warmth of Jack's skin on mine, the amber light cast on his bare muscular body from the roaring fireplace, the sweet smells of supper and Jack's aftershave as he pressed into me, in a pulse, the rise and fall of his body in perfect rhythm with mine. And finally a release as one soul. Love like I had never known wrapped me in warmth. I lifted my head and craned back exposing all of me to him in those intense seconds. It was the most perfect moment of my life.

I was home—safety and happiness washed over me like nothing I had ever felt.

CHAPTER 21

Jack and I had supper after we had dessert then headed in to decorate the oversized tree. The Fru Frus had left boxes and boxes of decorations all up the steps. Plus Jack had brought over a box too—an old box of tinsel we had found in the attic when we had fixed up the house back in September. Childhood memories were everywhere.

"Let's begin at the bottom and work our way up, Jack suggested opening his box first. "Why don't we lay everything out on the table in there and see what we have."

"Perfect! I agreed as I picked up my carton and headed to the dining room. Jack followed me, setting his box down on the floor. He squatted down to rekindle the fire. Just as he did, a sparkle of glitter coming from the mantle caught my eye. Another gift.

"Jack, here's what I've been talking about. Are you leaving me these? C'mon. It's you isn't it?"

"No. What are you talking about?"

"This." I showed him the little gold box with the red velvet bow. It was the same as all the others. I opened it and stood frozen. It was a pin. A silver lapel pin. It looked old. Like an antique. I was overcome. I felt my lip quiver.

"What is it, baby?"

"It's a dandelion."

Jack knew my story with my Granny. I had told him she thought they were all wishes just waiting to be made. I looked up at him and smiled.

"Who's leaving all the little surprises?

"I have no idea. But I love it," he said as he opened his box of decorations. "Maybe it's your mom—or your sister."

I attached the pin to my sweater and Jack and I kept working on the huge tree. He strung the lights like a pro. Mostly all white but the nostalgic part of me wanted a sprinkle of color. It added so much warmth. Jack had worked up a sweat. He removed his over-shirt and worked in his tight white tee-shirt. He looked scrumptious, his dark golden bangs falling over his baby face. That dimple made me hot all over again. He kinda looked like a young Kurt Russell. Sexy but with a baby face. He looked down from the ladder and smiled at me.

"Wanna play with my balls?" He said grinning, then dropping two satin balls down on top me. They bounced off my head.

"I thought I already did that tonight," I tossed it back.

"I'll have to put you on my naughty list," he popped.

"Oh, well, I've heard that's the best list to be on. Everybody knows if you're on the nice list you obviously aren't having a bit of fun."

Jack laughed and jumped down the ladder, dragging garland with him.

"Come here you—you're my best present." He laughed as he wrapped me in tinsel and white snowy garland. He was happy and so playful. We played Christmas carols and sang along, hung the old-fashioned popcorn strings I had made with my sisters earlier in the day and then we opened the old box of ornaments. My eyes immediately stung with salty tears. My life was inside that cardboard square. I took the items out slowly as not to damage anything, everything so precious and so full of emotion. A heart made of construction paper caught my eye. Inscribed in glitter around the edges were the simple words, "I love you Mom." I felt a tear escape and trickle down my cheek. I must've been in about third grade. Inside the red heart was my school picture from that year. I felt Jack's hand on my shoulder.

"You okay baby?" Then he saw what was in my hand. "Sweetheart. I'm so sorry. It will all happen in its own time. You can't force these things."

"I know. I was just pretty awful today."

"Wanna stop? We don't have to put these up now—or at all. We can leave this for later. But baby, this is where these decorations go—they tell the story of this house. Of your life. All of it."

I smiled at him. He was right. All of this belonged on this massive ridiculous oversized tree. I kept going, finding things we had made, little decorations from the St. Catherine's Christmas Bazaars of holidays past. I hung each item with love and care. Finding another, then another of the handmade ornaments soothed my soul in a way I couldn't describe, a feeling of joy and sadness all rolled into one. I wanted to get those happier times back. Maybe I could. I smiled to myself. A sudden feeling of happiness came over me. I had all the power I needed right here inside me. I could do anything I wanted. I owned this house.

"I love you, Jack Bennett," I said turning to him and kissing his luscious lips. "Thank you for being such a rock for me, for standing by me through everything over these last months. But I think we're fixin' to have us the best Christmas anybody's had in years!"

This was gonna be one Christmas we would never forget!

You are cordially invited to
The first annual Tuscaloosa Christmas Gala
At the new Southern Comforts Inn

Doors open at 7pm
Hors d'oeuvres will begin at 7:30pm

CHAPTER 22

The evening of the Gala had finally arrived. It was exactly one week before Christmas and Tuscaloosa was alive with the season. I was full of excitement and nerves. I knew that was normal but the girls and I had so much going on. We had planned the events down to the second to make sure we got Marci and put her right where she belonged. I had called her and told her she could keep her room—that Jack and I had thought about it and he would sign those phony papers when the party was over. She had checked in as scheduled the night before. Staying in the other bedrooms were Tuscaloosa's most elite, the mayor, Matt Walden, Nick Saban, the Alabama football coach and his wife, and several other dignitaries from the area.

I was standing at the front desk next to the ginormous tree Jack and I had decorated. Josie, my intern was running around helping to serve the hors d'oeuvres. Jack leaned in and kissed me and then headed into the front parlor to meet and greet. God he was so hot in his tux and crimson bowtie, his dark sandy hair pushed back over his forehead, subtle stripes of summer still glistening in the rich golden strands. His little square wire frames made him look even more delectable. Jack was wearing silver vintage cuff links on his crisp white shirt. They seemed to match the silver in those cute spectacles. He glanced over his shoulder as he sauntered away, winking at me, melting me.

"You ready for this?" Vivi asked with a twinkle in her eye. She was in a vintage dark Victorian red satin dress with an off-the-shoulder neckline. It was tea length and looked like it was right out of the late forties. Her lipstick matched it perfectly. She was stunning.

"Never been more ready for anything," I shot back with a wink. "You look fabulous! Stand back so I can get a look at you," Vivi said.

I was in a deep red velvet dress with a cream chiffon full skirt. Very vintage. My red satin pumps were perfectly matched. The bodice of the dress had a sweetheart neckline and my hair hung in bouncy waves pulled back loosely with baby's breath. I looked like I had snowflakes in my hair. I matched my house. I felt really beautiful for the very first time in as long as I could remember. And confident too. I pinned my dandelion jewel right on my dress at the shoulder. It was for Granny.

It was 7pm and the guests from upstairs were making their way down the staircase. Christmas music played in sophisticated tones from the front room across from the check in desk. The little five-piece orchestra was lovely, and perfect. They even had a harpist along with the other stringed instruments. We had the old grand piano refurbished and it was proudly in full use as the huge fireplace blazed in the background. I knew Daddy and Uncle Ron as well as Granny would all be so proud. Our house was alive again, filled with life and love and joy. And Christmas. Christmas was everywhere in this house. It's not just a time of year. It was my new state of mind. I finally felt like a grown-up. I owned my own life for the first time.

I had called Blake and Vivi along with Abby and Annie and told them about the real divorce papers that Jack had found. Then I called Dallas. I shouldn't have been shocked to learn that Marci had already called Dallas to give her a heads up about the accusations she planned to make—at my Gala. I could not believe it. But Marci had actually planned to do me in at the Christmas party, with all the most elite in Tuscaloosa right there to witness it all first hand. But Blake had it all worked out. Her husband Sonny is Tuscaloosa's police chief and he had staged a few choice officers on the grounds. Dallas was certainly gonna be here, but not to cover any wrong-doing...the Gala itself was the lead story, just like I had hoped. But she was gonna get footage to expose Marci and her uncle for a future story. We had all gotten together and planned the whole thing out, down to the second.

The wild card was Coco and those damn little people.

"Hi Judge McCullough," I greeted as Harlin and his gorgeous wife, Willow arrived. They were one of Tuscaloosa's first families. Of course Drew was there in a gorgeous three-piece suit.

"My goodness, you sure clean up nice, I said leaning in to give Drew a kiss on the cheek.

"And you my dear look like the queen of the ball, and of course you are," he smiled and kissed me back.

Outside, several Alabama football players were acting as valets, parking the cars in white bow ties and long tail tuxes. It was grand. Just as Judge McCullough stepped onto the porch and toward the open door, an elf burst in front of him.

"Good God almighty, where in hell did that little dude come from? Damn near scared the crap outta me," the judge exclaimed.

Without any warning the elf then performed the famous cartwheel and took out Willow with a foot to the boob. They had practiced that on me earlier in the week.

"Lawd have mercy, some damn body grab ahold of that...that...person. He's a danger. A flyin' weapon I tell ya. You alright baby?" Judge McCullugh asked Willow as they recovered. They glared at the little person as they made their way inside.

"Coco! Get those elves under control. Right this minute. That was the judge for God's sake. No more acrobats."

"What, but our routine is so full of flips, Rhonda. Look, I'll make sure they don't greet the guests with anymore flips or stunts, okay?"

"Okay, remember, classy, elegant. Those are your words for tonight. Repeat them over and over."

"Well, honey, I got just what you want then. Cue the Dickens carolers," he yelled to the side of the porch. And with that a very round lady in a dark green velvet dress, complete with hoop skirt and hand muff and bonnet lead the parade of singers, bursting out with Deck The Halls. The lady and the three men, in turn of the century tux and tails, strolled to the middle of the front yard and stopped near the sidewalk, to perform a little concert.

"Okay, that's much better," I concurred. "Just keep repeating, elegance, elegance, elegance, and you'll be just fine. I turned to go back inside when out the corner of my eye I caught Mother. Just then Vivi stepped up next to me. "Good God in heaven, your mother's date really is Santa Claus! How the hell did she hitch a ride in his sleigh?"

"I certainly do not want to even imagine the answer to that!" I retorted.

My mother was stepping out of a real sleigh, on tractor wheels of course. What else? She was grasping the hand of a handsome tuxedoed young man as her patent leather heel touched the pavement at the gate to the front lawn. A man in a bright red Santa suit stepped out next as mother took the arm Santa offered and headed up the sidewalk finally reaching me on the porch.

"Rhonda, thank you for the invitation. Here is my plus one. Meet Santa."

"Okay, I'll go with it. Nice to meet you... Santa." I looked at him as close as I could. I couldn't see anything but his eyes. I had to admit, I had no idea who she had brought with her. But once he stepped inside, he let out a huge Ho Ho Ho, and everyone turned. Mother was quite a piece of work. Now she had all of the attention. I was sure it had been her plan all along.

"Santa has arrived!" She announced with a massive smile. As the guest came over to say "hey" to Santa, Jean-Pierre poked his head from the kitchen.

"Rhonda, get in here quick," he motioned from the doorway, where a hint of smoke floated in behind him.

"Blake, watch the desk and greet people," I ordered as I headed into the back.

"Oh no, what happened?" I asked as I trotted in to see for myself. Jean-Pierre had opened the back door. My homemade eggnog was scorching. The smell was horrendous.

"What the hell?"

"And Honey, I hate to tell you but your balls are burnin.'"

"Well that's a new one. Quick, take 'em off the fire! Aww. My poor honey spicy meatballs. Damn! Oh well. Grab another batch out of the freezer and throw 'em in the oven fast. Open the door and let the smoke out.

Just then as I opened the back door to air out the kitchen, Mrs.

Galdys Haygood, the old sexpot from next door popped up on the back steps with her plus one.

"Hey Sweetie, well, I'm here with my date. And, as the smoke cleared, looking just like fog from a Vegas show, there stood a half-naked Chippendale dancer with a bare chest and a bowtie.

"Uhm, hey Gladys. Uhm, your date is gorgeous but he needs a shirt."

"Oh, well I had no idea this was a *no shirt no service* type a party. C'mon honey, you know it would be a sin to cover this hot bod." She ran her fingers up and down his rippled chest. Okay, she was at least seventy-five years old. I literally had no words. Just then Jack rushed in.

"Baby, Coco has asked that we all step outside to watch the routine."

I looked at him like I had forgotten for a moment where I was. Eyes bugged out— like I was hallucinating. My mouth dropped open, still trying to figure out how to introduce this half-naked dancer to the judge.

"You know," Jack pushed. "The dancing elves and all." He reiterated.

Oh God.

CHAPTER 23

We all made our way outside to the front porch and waited. The spotlight hit Coco first. Yes. They had rigged a spotlight. By the time Jack and I got there, both of us pushed in between Vivi and Blake who were already standing on the crowded front porch.

"Ladies and gentlemen, may I direct your attention to the side yard for this spectacular performance by none other than Santa's Elves." Coco motioned to the side of my house like he was announcing the Von Trapp Family Singers. Only this time, all the little performers showed up. The carolers began singing "We Are Santa's Elves," from the movie Rudolph the Red-nosed Reindeer, as all the little people bounded in turning flips and somersaults all between the lighted trees Drew had set up all over my front yard. They danced and twirled and lifted each other in the air.

But then the tossing began.

The spotlight flickered a few times causing one of the elves to miss catching his little elf brother.

"You freaking ass, you were supposed to catch me!" One screamed. And then all hell broke loose. An all out elf brawl right there in the middle of the first annual Tuscaloosa Christmas Gala.

"Coco! Do something!" I yelled.

"Stop! Stop it! Go back to your routine!" Coco tried. "They aren't listening, Rhonda. I don't know what to do."

All we could see in the flickering broken floodlight light was the little people all kicking at each other with their pointy curled green velvet elf shoes. The flashing light made it look like a strobe, a surreal freeze-framed super eight movie of the North Pole gone nuts.

"Go get me Santa. We need Santa!" Coco yelped." Like Santa was real and he could make the elves stop the battle.

Santa rounded the corner of the porch and ran to the front yard where the free-for-all had traveled. One elf swung from a tree branch and landed right on Santa's shoulders and began pulling at his beard. His fake beard. Santa struggled to get it back in place as the elf jumped down.

"Stop this right now. Or nobody gets paid!" Santa bellowed in a deep gravelly voice. "I said NOW!"

All of the little people froze in their tracks, some of them mid kick. The Victorian carolers had kept right on singing, so once everyone was quiet and the front yard was still, *We are Santa's Elves* took over in song once again. It was the last verse. Everyone from the party broke into applause, like all of this had been planned.

"Oh, that was just delightful, so entertaining dear," The mayor's wife bubbled as she clapped then turned to head back inside.

"That was hilarious, just totally made the evening for me," Mrs. Saban added. "Hell I might need those boys to run the ball for me next season. They're some fast little buggers," Nick said with a smile.

I peered over to the yard to see the elves and Santa bowing to the applause alongside the carolers. I glared at Coco. He smiled and blew me a kiss. Drew saw me and gave me a thumbs up.

"Well, that was—different," Jack whispered in my ear.

And nobody has to know."

Kinda like when you wet your pants," Vivi added.

I shook my head and swallowed hard. "I need a drink, how 'bout it?"

"My pleasure, m'lady, Jack said bowing in a tease.

"Something stiff," I begged.

"Like I said, my pleasure. I do aim to please," Jack said, with sarcasm and a wink, followed by a quick kiss on the cheek.

"When are we doing the deed?" Blake asked referring to the big Christmas gift we had planned for Marci.

"Oh very soon. Dallas and the live truck will be here any

minute."

Jack arrived with my drink and I threw back a swig like a sailor. Marci was wandering around like it was her party, meeting and greeting and hugging—but not for long.

"Isn't her Uncle coming by to pick her up for something?" Vivi remembered.

"Yep. Blake set that up. She sent him an invitation to a Tuscaloosa Lawyers Christmas party that wasn't real, of course, from an anonymous source. She knew he would take Marci as his date. She'd demand to go so she could be seen and search for a new rich husband," I explained.

"And looky who just got here, the low-life himself. I guess he's just gonna sit in the car out there in the street and wait for her. Oh look, Dallas is already here. She's out on the porch talking to Abby and Annie. Wonder when she got here?" Blake questioned.

"Okay we can do it now," I said clapping my hands together. "Grab everybody and get them to come to the dining room. Just the family. Not all the other guests. This is a private little party if you know what I mean. I'll get Marci. Blake you grab the gift."

I waited a few seconds watching all the right people file into the dining room and gather around the table. The huge, gorgeous wrapped gift sat in the middle like a centerpiece. It was covered in bright red striped paper with a big red bow. It looked wonderfully festive. A real surprise. I grinned to myself.

When Blake and Vivi, and her husband, Lewis, Abby and Annie, Sonny, along with Meridee and Jack and of course, Drew were all ready, I excused myself to the main parlor.

"Marci, could I see you for a second? I wanted you to know that I've talked to Jack. We don't want to keep this going a moment longer. I convinced him to sign your papers right now and we are glad to let you join us here at the inn."

"Really?" Marci seemed confused. But she smiled as I led her to the dining room.

"To welcome you to the family we all chipped in and bought you a Christmas present," I continued. Come on in here and open it up."

"Marci, I'm sorry. I know you just wanted me to sign. I'm happy if you're happy," Jack kept up the act.

Marci stood in front of her big surprise. Her black low cut satin dress swept the floor, even in her very high stilettos. She looked at all of us and smiled. "Thank y'all. I promise to be an asset to the inn. I'll give it my very best."

She pulled the ribbon off and separated the top from the box and sifting frantically through the tissue paper, her hand hit the envelope. She pulled it from the box. "Oh are these my deed papers to half of Jack's part of the property? Oooh I'm so excited," she oozed as she tore open the envelope and yanked the papers out. In her hand she held a copy of the real divorce papers, the ones she and Jack had both signed two years ago.

"Merry Christmas sweetheart!" Jack blared with a huge 'gotcha' grin.

"What are these?" Marci asked confused.

"We're divorced. We've been divorced. For years. And now, Blake, may I turn the honors over to you," Jack gestured as if introducing someone.

"Falsifying documents for immense personal gain is a crime punishable in all fifty states with fines and possible jail time. I know I have told you this already. Hope you love your new gift. We got you some new bracelets didn't we Sonny? Hope you love jewelry. Not so sure silver cuffs really go with that dress though." Blake smiled and moved back to let Sonny, her husband and Chief of Police, move in. Meridee winked at me and gave me a nod.

Sonny stepped toward her and read Marci her rights as one of his men cuffed her and led her out the back door. No one at the party even knew. Dallas had a cameraman standing in the corner getting everything for tomorrows broadcast when the crime report would air.

Outside, an officer already had her uncle in his squad car. Marci was escorted there and the car left as discreetly as it had arrived.

"They'll make bond and be released but this will sure put the fear of God in them." Sonny grinned as he popped an olive from the bar in his mouth and meandered back to the party.

"It sure helps to sleep with the chief of police," Blake winked.

"Oh baby, it's all over. It's all over." I let out a breath of anxiety and nerves and knew now Jack and I would finally have the Christmas we wanted. Jack picked me up and swung me around and around all the way out into the foyer.

"She's gone," he said. "We did it! I love you Rhonda!"

Just then, the crinoline under my skirt caught a tree branch and as he twirled me the tree began to fall, in slow motion. Jack yanked me hard and freed me fast, pulling me into the front parlor just as the entire tree came down into the bannister

"Oh my God! Is everybody okay?" He screeched.

"Fine!" I heard a little voice squeal from under the tree. Never been better."

Sonny, Lewis and Jack all ran and lifted the big tree only to find Gladys with her date, the half-naked dancer on top of her.

"You go, Gladys!" Meridee laughed.

"Honey, I'm in no hurry to move, so take your sweet time." Gladys giggled.

"Well, I guess it's not a party till the Christmas tree falls over," Vivi chuckled.

CHAPTER 24

The party had slowed and it was nearing midnight. It had been such a success. Moments after we stood the tree upright again, Dallas began her live broadcast for the ten o'clock news. After she finished, she and her husband, Cal Hollingsworth, joined in the revelry, playing the piano. Cal, Jack and Lewis had all been Alabama football stars and the good friendship was still evident as they all sang old carols around the bar. The drinks flowed and Jean-Pierre kept the food coming. Coco sent the elves and carolers home right after Dallas had them all on TV. It had been a night of dreams and I was exhausted and elated all at the same time.

After everyone had left, and most of the place had been straightened up, I hugged my sisters and Blake and Vivi goodnight.

"We'll be here tomorrow right after lunch to help you finish getting it all cleaned up." Blake promised as she walked to her car with Sonny.

"Okay, see y'all then. I really appreciate that," I hollered after her. "And thanks for everything tonight. I really mean that."

"My pleasure, Rhonda. It's what I love to do—get the losers off the streets. Now get some sleep." Sonny waved over the back of his head as he spoke.

Most of the guests were checking out at eleven the next morning. We had the main areas cleaned and Jean-Pierre and I had breakfast already to go. In the morning, all we had to do was heat it all up on the buffet with the chafing dishes. Simple. Breakfast would come early so I had hired a young sous-chef to come in and set up and serve till I could get downstairs.

I closed the door and let out a huge sigh as the final guest left.

"We did it," I smiled to Jack.

"You are the most amazing woman I have ever known," he murmured to me as he kissed me and headed upstairs. "Come soon. I'll be waiting to tuck you in," he grinned.

"I'll be right up. I just need to check and make sure everything's off in the kitchen." I headed into the cozy spot, finding it empty, cleaned and dark-- all except for a tiny light in the powder room. The door was cracked. I thought Jean-Pierre might be in there but as I got closer I could see Santa's red suit reflecting in the mirror over the sink. I could see him working on his beard. I moved closer. Curiosity had gotten the better of me. I wanted to know who this strange man at my party was—and why he was on the arm of my mother. I hid next to the bathroom door and peeked inside. Underneath the fake white beard, a real red stubbly beard was hiding. Santa removed the white beard and took off the red furry hat. He turned on the water at the sink and washed his face, grabbing a hand towel, he dried his skin. My heart stopped. Could it be? No I was sure it wasn't –was it? I squinted my eyes to see the refection in the mirror better.

"Uncle Ron, is that you?"

"Rhonda? What are you doing in here?" Mother blurted from behind me.

"Mother! I thought you left."

I was frozen. My throat closed and my stomach dropped to the floor. "Is it him? Is it Uncle Ron?" I stared, unbelievingly at my mother. He kinda looked like Gus, the gardener. I was confused.

The man that had just saved my party from an elf war stepped from inside the tiny bathroom. He held the hat and beard in his hands as he emerged quietly into the kitchen.

Uncle Ron spoke. "No, sweetheart, you aren't confused. It's me. Uncle Ron." He smiled weakly, not sure how I would accept him after all these years.

How? Uhm, where? Mother? When..." I couldn't form sentences.

"Sit down sweetie. I want to talk to you," Mother said.

My mouth was dry. I needed a drink.

"That day I came by to bring some new ornaments, I wanted to ask you about having a Santa for your party. We didn't know the right time to tell you."

"You think now was the perfect time?" I asked still in shock.

"Not really but this is how it happened. I wanted to be here to watch you at your big coming out. I'm so very, very proud of you, Rhonda. I always have been," Uncle Ron began to tear up. This was the way I could watch you and you wouldn't know it was me. I have wanted to tell you for so long, since you got the house after Don died. But I didn't know when or how. I called your mother and broke the news to her. I disappeared years ago because my brother wouldn't speak to me after he found out. I knew I had to leave your mother alone. She was doing the best she could."

I was swept away to the thought of all those cards I had found in the attic from him to my mother. How he begged to see me. How he begged to be part of our lives. I felt so sad for him. I jumped up and hugged him. I held him for so long, long enough for him to know I loved him deeply, long enough for him to know how much I missed him and needed him and long enough for him to know I didn't blame him. We held each other in the still quiet of the kitchen and sobbed. It felt so good to have him in my arms, to feel his protective arms around me, to smell that familiar smell of my childhood in his skin. He was sobbing for all the years we had missed. I opened my eyes for a second and glanced at Mother. Tears were streaming down her face. I reached my hand to her and she grabbed it back squeezing hard. I hated her and loved her at the same time. She had intercepted a lifetime of love and experiences I could have had with this man. But suddenly I understood.

What else could she have done? Any choice she could have made would have terrible consequences. She didn't want to split up our family. I guess she could have stopped her affair with my father's only brother—but how can you help who you fall in love with? Obviously these two really loved each other. Here they were—together after everything that had happened. I could finally see my mother. She didn't do any of the things she did because she loved me any less. All those secrets had actually been because she loved us all so much. She didn't want us to be hurt because of her actions. But Uncle Ron was the man she loved. She must have felt so guilty all these years.

I pulled back and looked at my uncle, my father. "I have your eyes," I said smiling.

"I love you. I love you so much. I wanted so badly to tell you back in September. But I hadn't even told your mother I had come back to town yet. All I could do was make you that dandelion garden. Mama would have loved that too."

"I always sit out there and think of Granny. I loved her so. That's our place you made out there. I sit and talk to Granny in my pretty pink chairs you made. I knew that Gus guy seemed to know me too well." He and Mother laughed.

I sat down next to mother in the banquette chair and reached over to her, laying my hand on top of hers. She was still tearing. I grabbed a napkin from the table drawer and handed it to her. Suddenly all the anger I had felt, all the animosity melted away. I could see her. The woman holding my hand was flawed. She had made mistakes. So many mistakes. She was human. Just a woman. I suddenly saw her as three dimensional. Maybe we don't see our mothers this way. As real people. We hold them up in some higher regard as super human. They are supposed to be better than us, have a higher mission. After all they are raising wonder women of their own. Us. To see our mother as flawed somehow might mean we are flawed too. We are. We just don't want to see our mothers this way. They are meant to be perfect. So we can say our mothers are so wonderful. But really they are just women, filled with mistakes and ragged around the edges from rolling with life's punches. My mother was just a woman. And suddenly, I loved her more than I ever had. I loved her deeply. I had to let that sink in. But best of all, I had forgiven her in those last few minutes and didn't even realize all those tears were a lifetime of anger melting away.

Forgiveness was a powerful thing. It was a gift that you gave yourself. The best Christmas gift I could have ever gotten.

"I understand Mother. I love you," I managed.

"What is that?" Mother asked looking at my dandelion pin.

"Oh, I've been finding these little boxes all around the house this week. This was the third one. All of them had something to do with a dandelion."

I looked at Ron as he grinned at my mother. "It was you? All of these were from you?"

"I wasn't sure when we were gonna tell you about me but I liked seeing you surprised. I wanted to give you a Christmas full of gifts."

I smiled and threw my arms around his neck. "Oh Uncle Ron. I guess there really is a Santa Claus. You. You are my Christmas present." My mother stood up and hugged me still sniffling. Then I reached around both of them. My parents.

I looked at my mother and kissed her cheek. "This is the best gift you ever got me. A real live Santa Clause—and a father all in one."

The End

EPILOGUE

New Years Day was sunny; crisp and cold. Frost covered the barren ground. It looked like a winter wonderland outside. Jack had stayed over—we had a New Years Eve in, ordered take-out, watched movies in silly fuzzy socks, drank spiked hot chocolate and snuggled in front of the bedroom fireplace all night. Jack had made plans for a special day for just the two of us today. I was excited and giddy. Jack was downstairs gathering food for a picnic. Yes, I said picnic. He had someplace he just knew would be warm enough for outdoor dining. I was game.

The inn was closed until Valentines Day so I had some much needed time off. I showered and got ready, sliding into my jeans and a nubby oversized white sweater with my crimson wool scarf. I pulled on my boots, spritzed myself with my Dior perfume and skipped down the stairs. Jack met me at the front door, telling me to go out that way. He didn't even want me to see what he had packed in the car. He went out the back door and rolled the car back enough to pick me up and we were off—to an undisclosed private location for our own New Years celebration.

"What do you think we're doin'," he asked, teasing me.

"You are kidnapping me and we're running away with only enough sustenance to last a few days. Then we'll have to snuggle for days to stay warm till someone finds us?"

"Close," he grinned.

Jack jumped up on the interstate heading toward Birmingham.

About half way, he took a side road that wound around through the woods, deeper and deeper until we hit a two-lane road. A wooden running fence, weather beaten and falling in led the way to a cluster of trees.

Suddenly a flood of memories came rushing back. I could hear water rushing, the gristmill churning from the far right side deep into a thicket. We turned into Tannehill State park, where I kissed a young gorgeous, gangly boy named Jack Bennett when I was barely fourteen. He was swinging across the creek on a vine, splashed into the water in front of me and within seconds, kissed me while we were under water. He called himself Tarzan in every love letter he wrote to me because he had to swing on a vine to get across the creek to meet me.

Before I knew it, Jack had pulled up to the edge of the creek. Tears filled my eyes as I got out, images of a skinny innocent girl danced across my mind as I stared at the muddy water, the old vine, now a rope, barely visible.

"Sit down here," Jack said smiling. He had put a red wool blanket on the bank of the creek. He sat down and patted the spot where he wanted me. I slowly sat down next to him and nestled into his arms. It was cold but the sun had begun to make it bearable. The warmth of Jack's body made me forget I ever even felt a chill. The creek was still—the trees barely moving. The quiet was mesmerizing and made for a perfect moment for the past to reappear, Jack with his boyish soft face tanned with just a splash of freckles across his nose, leaning in and kissing me, us bobbing up from under the water, giggling. We kissed dozens of times once we discovered each other's lips. He had wrapped around his finger for lifetime. It just took me a lifetime to find him again.

"I love you, Rhonda. I have never loved anyone else like I love you. Never. I know I never will. You are the other half of me. My Jane to your Tarzan," he grinned.

I suddenly knew this wasn't really a picnic. My heart raced hopeful, nervous, excited as Jack got on one knee and faced me.

"It has taken years to find you again. I was so afraid I'd never ever find you. But I never gave up. I never forgot how it felt to hold you, to kiss you, to have you next to me—you make me want to be better—to be the man you deserve. And no matter what I will never deserve the woman you are. I feel like the world is perfect when you are lying next to me, in my arms. My world is perfect again. Just like when I was fifteen, you are all I have ever needed. All I will ever need. Will you please, be my Jane and do me the biggest honor and marry me?"

I could barely speak; the knot in my throat was choking me. It was the single greatest moment of my entire life.

"Yes, Tarzan, Yes, I'll be your Jane, forever." And with that Jack pulled out a blue Tiffany box and opened it, a perfect square cut diamond ring in a vintage setting faced me. The inscription read: *To my perfect Jane, forever, Tarzan.* We were getting married. Jack Bennett was mine. All mine. Finally.

Now, The End.

Holiday Recipes

From

The Southern Comforts Inn

Whiskey Cookies

2 eggs
¾ c. sugar
2 c. flour
½ c. molasses
1 lb. pecans
1 box raisins (rolled in flour)
1 ½ Tbsp. water
1 ½ tsp. baking soda
1 ½ tsp. ground cloves
1 ½ tsp. cinnamon
1 ½ tsp. nutmeg
¼ c. whiskey

Mix all ingredients. (Roll raisins in flour before adding to mixture) Drop by teaspoon on greased cookie sheet. Bake at 350 degrees for 12 minutes.

Toni Henderson Smith

Hot Apple Cider

2 quarts (4 cups) of apple cider
(if u can't find that, I use plain apple juice)
1 1/2 quarts (3 cups) cranberry juice
1/2 cup brown sugar
1/2 tsp. salt
4 cinnamon sticks (I usually use about 6)
1/2 tsp. whole cloves (I usually use about 1 1/2 tsp.)

Mix all together in a big pot, bring to a boil, turn off, put lid on pot
and let it steep all day

Note: If company is coming, pour in a big crock pot to keep warm

Also Note: When it cools down, I usually pour it into the empty
containers the juices were in, add a cinnamon stick and cloves into
each container and put in fridge. Then when u want just 1 or 2 cups at
a time, pour from the jugs, microwave.

Sonya Durrett

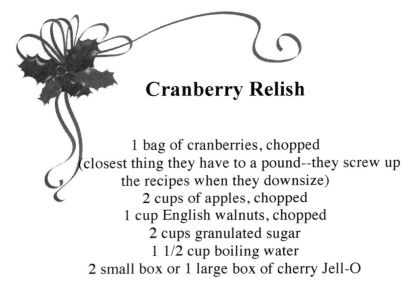

Cranberry Relish

1 bag of cranberries, chopped
(closest thing they have to a pound--they screw up
the recipes when they downsize)
2 cups of apples, chopped
1 cup English walnuts, chopped
2 cups granulated sugar
1 1/2 cup boiling water
2 small box or 1 large box of cherry Jell-O

Combine sugar, water, Jell-O and dissolve. Add nuts, cranberries, and apples--stir. Put into your favorite serving dish--mine is a real pretty, glass antique footed bowl. Put in refrigerator until firm--several hours. Don't forget to put plastic wrap over the top to keep it safe.

Denise Holcomb

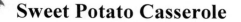

Sweet Potato Casserole

6 or 8 sweet potatoes, peeled and cutinto 1-inch cubes
3/4 cup packed brown sugar
1/4 cup butter, softened
1 1/2 teaspoons salt
1/2 teaspoon vanilla extract
1/2 cup finely chopped pecans, divided
Cooking spray
2 cups miniature marshmallows

Preparation
Preheat oven to 375°.
Place the sweet potatoes in a large pot, and cover with cold water.
Bring to a boil. Reduce heat, and simmer for 15 minutes or until very
tender. Drain; cool slightly.

Place potatoes in a large bowl. Add next 4 ingredients. Mash sweet
potato mixture with a potato masher. Fold in 1/4 cup pecans. Scrape
potato mixture into an even layer in an 11 x 7-inch baking dish coated
with cooking spray. Sprinkle with remaining 1/4 cup pecans; top with
marshmallows. Bake at 375° for 25 minutes or until golden.

Billie Williams Nelson

Hattie's Multi Use Pie Filling

(We use it every holiday!)
1 cup sugar
1 cup milk
2 eggs separated
3 T. Flour mixed in very warm water
Pinch of salt
1t. Vanilla
Reserve egg whites for meringue
Mix all ingredients together and bring to a boil. Cook until thick while stirring often.
For Chocolate Pie Filling add 3 T. Cocoa powder mixed in a little warm water and stir.
For Coconut Pie Filling add 1 T. of coconut and stir.
For Banana pudding pour over layers of vanilla wafers and bananas.
For Meringue beat the egg whites till stiff. Stir in 3T of sugar and beat again until stiff and white. Spread over pies or pudding and bake until golden brown.
This recipe uses 9 inch pie shells. The mixture can also be used to make chocolate pudding by adding cocoa and skipping the shell.

Connie Hunnicutt Stringer

Refrigerator Fruitcake

1 can Angel Flake Coconut
1 can Eagle Brand Milk
1 large box Vanilla Wafers
8 oz red candied cherries
8 oz green candied cherries
1 qt of pecans, chopped

Crush vanilla wafers into a fine consistency, this can be done in a food processor or blender. Cut cherries into smaller pieces. Mix crushed vanilla wafers with Eagle Brand Milk. Add coconut, cherries and pecans. Form into a log or rectangle using wax paper, cover and refrigerate. Refrigerate overnight or for several hours then slice and enjoy!

Gail Estes Hollingsworth

Christmas Punch

I bottle apple juice or apple cider
I small bag red hot candies
Heat until candy is melted
Serve warm

Kay Finch Swindle

Cranberry Swiss Cheese Ball

A bit sharp and a bit sweet with a tang.
Wonderful on crackers or toasted flat bread squares.
8 oz Swiss cheese, grated (like Jarlsberg)
4 oz cream cheese (can use low fat)
3 TBSP mayonnaise (can use low fat)
¼ tsp nutmeg
¼ tsp white pepper
2 tsp dried lemon zest

With electric mixer or food processor, blend together until creamy. Add ¼ cup chopped dried cranberries and mix in. (Can substitute fresh chopped cranberries, diced maraschino cherries or chopped red and green candied cherries for a holiday look)

Form two balls or one large ball. Wrap in plastic wrap and refrigerate several hours, until firm. Unwrap and roll each ball in chopped pecans or sliced almonds. Wrap balls in plastic wrap. Refrigerate at least one hour before serving. Can be made several days or a week ahead. Keep wrapped. Flavors will enhance with time. *This basic recipe of grated cheese, cream cheese and mayonnaise can be altered to create many yummy cheese balls or spreads. For spreads, use a softer cheese and/or increase mayonnaise to 1/2 cup. Use any kind of cheese and addition of chopped dried fruit or diced peppers, olives and/or spices. For those sensitive to nuts, leave off nuts. Can roll in sunflower seeds, chopped pumpkin seeds or chopped peanuts. For a sweet dessert cheese roll, can roll in chocolate sprinkles or red and/or green sugar sprinkles. Great with fresh apple slices or paired with fresh apple cider, sparkling cider, hot, spiced cider, or a favorite wine.

Gail Estes Hollingsworth

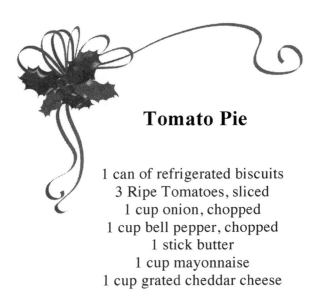

Tomato Pie

1 can of refrigerated biscuits
3 Ripe Tomatoes, sliced
1 cup onion, chopped
1 cup bell pepper, chopped
1 stick butter
1 cup mayonnaise
1 cup grated cheddar cheese

Sauté onions and pepper in butter, set aside mix mayonnaise and cheese, set aside Roll out 5 biscuits in pie plate for crust. Top with half of onions and peppers, add tomatoes, top with remaining onion mixture. Then top with cheese mixture. Top with remaining biscuits. Bake at 350 until brown. 8-10 servings.

Faye Hubbard

Corn Casserole

1 can whole kernel corn, drained
1 can creamed corn
2 eggs beaten
1 stick butter, melted
4 heaping T. all purpose flour
2 T. sugar
1/4 C. diced green pepper (you can use red, I only had green)
1 C. whole milk
1/2 C. shredded cheddar cheese
1/4 tsp each salt and pepper

Combine all ingredients and pour into a greased casserole dish. Bake at 350 degrees for 1 hr. 20 min.

Ingredients:
8 ounces cream cheese, softened
2 cups sour cream (I used light)
1 1/2 cups shredded cheddar cheese
6 slices bacon, cooked and crumbled
1/2 cup sliced green onion

Instructions:
Preheat oven to 400 F.
Combine softened cream cheese, sour cream, cheddar cheese, bacon and green onion. Spoon mixture into a 1-quart baking dish and bake for 25-30 minutes, or until cheese is bubbling and hot.

Serve with bread slices, crackers, or veggies

Yvette Dooley Miller

MAGIC COOKIE BARS

1 ½ cups corn flake crumbs
3 T sugar
1 stick melted butter or margarine
1 cup (6oz. pkg.) semi-sweet chocolate morsels
1 1/3 cups (3 ½ oz. can) flaked coconut
1 cup coarsely chopped walnuts
1 can sweetened condensed milk

Mix corn flake crumbs and sugar in 12 x 9 in. baking pan, then add butter and mix all together. With back of tablespoon, press mixture evenly and firmly in bottom of pan to form crust.

Scatter chocolate morsels over crust. Spread coconut evenly over morsels. Sprinkle walnuts over coconut. Pour sweetened condensed milk evenly over top of layers.

Bake in moderate oven, 350 degrees, about 25 minutes or until lightly browned around edges. Cool. Cut into pieces.

Makes approximately 54 pieces depending on how large pieces are cut.

Patsy Bruce

COCKTAIL MEATBALLS

Meatballs: 2 lbs. ground beef
1 cup bread crumbs
2 T instant onions
1 egg
Salt and pepper
Make into 1" meatballs. Cook and drain. These can be made ahead
of time and frozen until needed.

Sauce: In frying pan, put **one large jar of grape jelly** and add **one bottle of chili sauce.** Heat together; add meatballs and coat with sauce.

Serve in a chaffing dish under low heat.

Patsy Bruce

Divinity Fudge

2 1/2 cups sugar
½ cup corn syrup
2 egg whites
2/3 cup water
1 ½ cup chopped nuts
1 Tablespoon vanilla
1/8 teaspoon salt

Cook sugar syrup salt and water until a small amount forms a soft ball, (234-240 degrees) when tested in cold water. Take our ½ cup of this mixture and cook the rest until it forms a hard ball, (250-265 degrees) when tried in cold water. Pour the half cup of water slowly over the beaten egg whites. Beat constantly. Continue beating and add the remainder of the syrup. Add nuts and vanilla and keep beating until mass thickens and becomes heavy. Pour into buttered pan and cut when cold or drop with a teaspoon.

Rita Lewis Holifield

Southern Cornbread Dressing

Bread for dressing:
2 Cups self-rising corn meal
1 Cup self-rising flour
Mix the two up well then add
4 eggs
¼ cup cooking oil

Pour enough buttermilk over this to mix it up. Then add a little water to it to make it a bit soupie. Pour into greased cast iron skillet at 450 degrees till browned.

Don't make this ahead of time. Make it just before you make the dressing.

DRESSING:
Crumble cornbread after it is cool enough to handle into a large bowl.
Add:
½ Cup of celery
1 Cup of chopped onion
Mix well and add chicken or turkey broth. Mix well until mushy.
Salt and pepper to taste
Cook in oven at 400 degrees until lightly browned.

Joyce Albright Jones

Beth's Holiday Turkey Baste

1 Cup pure maple syrup
2 sticks butter, melted
Mix all together, melted and warm
and pour into a bowl.

Pre-baste the turkey with butter salt and pepper on the outside and put
inside oven bag. Cook your turkey the way you usually cook it. I go
by the weight and instructions on the bag. Every twenty minutes baste
the turkey, shooting this mixture inside and under the skin. Each time
also use some of the turkey's own juices to mix in with this. You can
also use chicken broth just help keep the turkey moist. I repeat this
until the turkey comes out of the oven and baste with this mixture one
more time before we carve the bird. Tastes so delicious I barely have
any turkey leftover.

Beth Albright

Meet Beth Albright

 Beth Albright is a Tuscaloosa native, former Days of Our Lives actress, and former radio and TV talk show host. She is a graduate of the University of Alabama School of Journalism. She is also a screenwriter, voice-over artist and mother. She is the mother of the most wonderful brilliant son in the universe, Brooks and is married to her college sweetheart, Ted. A perpetually homesick Southern Belle and a major Alabama Crimson Tide fan, she splits her time between San Francisco and, of course, Tuscaloosa.

Beth loves to connect with her readers.

Visit her online:
www.bethalbrightbooks.com

Facebook:
https://www.facebook.com/authorbethalbright

Twitter:
https://twitter.com/BeththeBelle

Goodreads:
https://www.goodreads.com/author/show/6583748.Beth_Albright

Made in the USA
Lexington, KY
02 July 2015